A beam of [light swept across the] field and illuminated both humans and plants. As fast as it appeared, it was gone.

"What was that?" Didi whispered urgently to Allie.

"A car beam, coming off the road. Shh! Listen."

Didi heard a low, quiet throbbing. And then it was gone, like the beam of light.

"Turned the ignition off," Allie whispered. Luckily his expertise as a police officer was coming in handy.

Didi clutched the flashlight tightly. She stood absolutely straight up, still, like a cornstalk. Allie bent down gingerly and pulled the weapon from his ankle holster. Then he stood straight . . . like Didi, in an exaggerated posture.

They heard nothing for five paralyzing minutes. And then the soft, slow crunch of footsteps in the garden. They seemed faraway.

Didi dropped her head and closed her eyes. The excitement, the anticipation, the fear, made her woozy. Now the crunching steps were closer, much closer. A minute later came a dull thud. Then another one. . . .

MYSTERY FAVORITES

Dr. Nightingale Goes to the Dogs

A DEIRDRE QUINN
NIGHTINGALE
MYSTERY

Lydia Adamson

A SIGNET BOOK

SIGNET
Published by the Penguin Group
Penguin Books USA Inc., 375 Hudson Street,
New York, New York 10014, U.S.A.
Penguin Books Ltd, 27 Wrights Lane,
London W8 5TZ, England
Penguin Books Australia Ltd, Ringwood,
Victoria, Australia
Penguin Books Canada Ltd, 10 Alcorn Avenue,
Toronto, Ontario, Canada M4V 3B2
Penguin Books (N.Z.) Ltd, 182–190 Wairau Road,
Auckland 10, New Zealand

Penguin Books Ltd, Registered Offices:
Harmondsworth, Middlesex, England

First published by Signet, an imprint of Dutton Signet,
a division of Penguin Books USA Inc.

First Printing, February, 1995
10 9 8 7 6 5 4 3 2 1

 REGISTERED TRADEMARK—MARCA REGISTRADA

Printed in the United States of America

PUBLISHER'S NOTE
This is a work of fiction. Names, characters, places, and incidents either are
the product of the author's imagination or are used fictitiously, and any resem-
blance to actual persons, living or dead, events, or locales is entirely
coincidental.

Chapter 1

Didi stood up and stepped away from Lucifer. Lucifer was a six-and-a-half-month-old Duroc pig. Of the breed they used to call Jersey Reds—hearty, fast-growing, intelligent.

She stripped the examining gloves from her hands and let the gloves drop to the ground.

Deirdre Quinn Nightingale, DVM, was angry. Very, very angry.

She stared at Ledeen, the man who owned the pig. Then she stared at Charlie Gravis, her geriatric veterinary assistant, who had persuaded her to come out to examine Lucifer.

"Do you mind, Mr. Ledeen, if I confer privately with my assistant?" she asked with exaggerated formality.

"Hell no," said Ledeen. He was a tall, gangly man with a ponytail. He wore a flannel shirt beneath his overalls even though it was a warm day. Except for his neatly kept goatee, his face was clean shaven, and heavily scarred. His eyes were deep set and constantly moving.

"Thank you, Mr. Ledeen," Didi replied and walked out of the makeshift pen, motioning for Charlie Gravis to follow.

When they were out of Ledeen's earshot, Didi stripped off her weathered jumpsuit, revealing a handsome pale yellow dress with a high collar and long sleeves. She folded the dirty outer garment carefully.

"Are you feeling okay, Charlie?" she asked.

"Just fine, Miss," he replied.

"You *do* know what day it is, don't you, Charlie?"

"Yes, Miss. Your birthday. July thirtieth."

"Right. And you *do* know what is going on today, don't you, Charlie? In about an hour or so."

"A party, Miss. Your birthday party."

"But it's not just any birthday party—right, Charlie? It's the first party of any kind that I've given since I came back to Hillsbrook. It's the first time our neighbors and friends have come to the house since my mother died. Isn't that right, Charlie?"

"Right, Miss."

"So it's not just a silly old birthday party, is it, Charlie? It's something special. It's something I'm doing because of a whole lot of hurt and pride in my heart, Charlie. It's about my mother. Do you understand that, Charlie?"

"Yes, Miss."

"And we've all been very busy preparing for this. And I still have to get the ice and I have to pick up Mary Hyndman at her place and take her to the party because she's too infirm now to drive."

"I know all that, Miss."

"If you know all that, Charlie—why did you get me out here on this fool's errand? You said it was an emergency. What kind of emergency, Charlie? Where is the emergency? Is the world going to come to an end because Lucifer is just not interested in the two sows in heat that Ledeen penned on either side of him? Is that your emergency, Charlie? Is that why you dragged me all the way out here?"

"He was very upset on the phone. He was calling from the gas station," Charlie explained. And then he added, "And he's kin."

"Kin!"

"Yes, Miss. Kin."

"A twelfth cousin on your uncle's side? Is that it, Charlie?" Didi clenched and unclenched her fists and stared down at the shoes that she had forgotten to change. They were covered with mud.

It was futile to get angry with Charlie, she thought, but she couldn't help herself. Kin! All four of the nice misfits she had inherited from her mother—Charlie and Mrs. Tunney and Abigail and Trent Tucker—were all "kin." Whatever that meant. Sooner or later everyone was everyone else's cousin. She stared past Charlie to the obviously unhappy Mr. Ledeen. She could tell he was poor and desperate. But everyone who lived on the Ridge was poor and desperate. They all lived, like Mr. Ledeen, in trailers set up on cinder blocks, without hot water or electricity or phones. The Ridge was Hillsbrook's Tobacco Road. As Hillsbrook, itself, had become more affluent, more suburban, the Ridge had grown poorer. People of the Ridge raised pigs to survive—to eat.

Didi walked over to Mr. Ledeen, who did a

double take when he noticed her outfit. He was confused by her transformation from farmhand to belle of the ball.

"There's nothing the matter with Lucifer," she said simply.

"The hell there ain't," Ledeen snapped. "He ain't gruntin, he ain't salivatin, and there's two pretty young things on either side of him all hot to go. Don't tell me there ain't nothing the matter with him."

"Mr. Ledeen!" Didi said sharply, assuming her role as Doctor Nightingale, DVM, the ultimate authority of all things animal. "I have examined your boar very carefully. There is no brucellosis or osteomalacia or arthritis. The testicles, epididymides, and scrotum are fine. Locomotor function is fine. You just have to be patient with Lucifer. Some boars achieve sexual maturity later than others. It's as simple as that."

"He's old enough, he is. Six and a half month. I ain't never had a boar who couldn't do it at six and a half month. But it ain't a question of him not being able to do it—he don't *want* to do it."

"It is quite common for boars to remain sexually immature until they are eight months of age, Mr. Ledeen. In fact, there are some large-scale pig farming operations that won't use a boar before he reaches eight months."

Ledeen shook his head stubbornly. "No. You gotta take a whaddayacallit—a semen sample. Send it to the lab. Gotta do that. Something bad is wrong with Lucifer."

Didi glared at the man. She was astonished

at his arrogance. Everybody knew that Ledeen
didn't have a dime to pay for anything. Didi
knew this was going to be a free visit, that it
would be useless even to send Ledeen a bill.
And now he wanted complicated procedures
and lab work done for a pig that was perfectly healthy.

"I am going to give that some consideration,
Mr. Ledeen," Didi said, "but right now I have
another client waiting."

"Charlie!" Ledeen shouted. "This is no way
to treat kin."

Didi struggled to keep her cool.

"Tell me, Mr. Ledeen," she said, "are there
any heritable defects in Lucifer's line?"

"Say what?"

"Did his daddy have a scrotal hernia?"

"His daddy was a damn tiger."

"Then Lucifer, too, will become one, no
doubt—in forty-five days or so. And there is
no need whatever to evaluate his semen, Mr.
Ledeen. Now—Good day!"

She walked briskly back to the red jeep.
Charlie Gravis fell into step behind her.

"Do we get ice first?" Charlie asked once
they were on the road.

"No. We get Mary Hyndman first, Charlie."
Didi spoke gently, having decided not to
broach the subject of Ledeen's unamorous pig
ever again.

She drove more slowly than usual because
she was heading toward Mary's cottage without locational confidence. The way was not really clear. It had been nine months since she
had gone to see Mary, and that was the first

and last time she had ever been to the cottage.
It had been a professional visit: to put down
Mary's last remaining German shepherd—a
bitch named Raymonda who could no longer
see or walk.

Mary herself had already become infirm. She
got around on a walker. But, after all, Mary
was close to ninety. Didi had sent her an invi-
tation to the birthday party but had never expected a reply. The reply did come, however,
and promptly. Yes, Mary had said she would
like to attend—if someone could come and
pick her up, because she could no longer manage the car.

Everyone was astonished that Mary Hyndman wanted to come to the party under any
circumstances. She had been a virtual recluse
since her husband's death ten years ago.

"I remember that beat-up old sycamore
tree," Didi noted. She accelerated, sure of the
way now.

They were close to the cottage. Didi felt
good. It was a rare pleasure to see Mary. And
the old woman would understand the importance of the party. She was a wise lady. Didi's
mother had always confided in Mary. Everyone had, until she withdrew from all her
friends.

Mary was tall—almost six feet—with a kind
of hunched back and a beautiful face. Her hair
was always long and loose. Her husband had
been affiliated with one of those international
foundations that dispensed disaster aid. He
and Mary were always off to Malaysia or north-

east Brazil or Ethiopia after an earthquake or war.

Mary was also a legendary gardener and in the early 1960s had published a book, *The Complete Garden*, in which she had argued that flowers and vegetables should be grown together in the same soil. The exquisite photographs and detailed instructions in the book then demonstrated how to plant and manage such a garden.

"Right here!" Didi said happily and turned the jeep off the main road and onto the narrow dirt path that led to the Hyndman place.

"Look out!" Charlie yelled.

Didi swerved at the same time the oncoming green station wagon swerved. Luckily the swerves were coordinated.

Both vehicles squealed to a stop.

"Sorry!" Didi called out to the large redheaded and red bearded man behind the wheel.

Then she noticed the "MD" plates on his car. Quickly she climbed out of the jeep and approached him. "Is Mary okay?"

"She's fine," the doctor answered. "She had a fall. But nothing's broken."

"What happened to Dr. Fisk?" Didi asked, remembering the name of the doctor that Mary had spoken about during that sad visit when Raymonda was put down.

"He's on vacation. I'm covering for him. I'm Dr. Purdy, from Dover Plains."

He started his engine. "You ought to make a wider turn next time so you can see if another vehicle is coming down the path," he counseled pompously.

Didi just nodded. He was right. Irritating but right.

"By the way," Dr. Purdy called as he drove off, "I left the front door open so the puppy could go in and out. Those were Mrs. Hyndman's instructions." He turned onto the main road and vanished from sight.

Didi was taken aback for a moment. Had she heard right—*a puppy*? She turned to Charlie, who was still in his seat and obviously still a little shaken from the near-collision.

"Did he say Mary had a puppy?"

"That's what I heard, Miss."

Didi got back into the jeep, shaking her head. "Tell me, Charlie, how she can manage a puppy when she can't even manage herself."

Charlie only shrugged.

Didi parked by the fenced-in, overgrown garden that adjoined Mary's cottage. She could smell the radishes and scallions growing through the weeds.

As she headed for the front door, which the good doctor had indeed left open for the sake of the puppy, Didi laughed a little wickedly and pointed to the garden fence.

"Look, Charlie," she said, "the woman is past ninety and she still makes a better scarecrow than you."

The big, brooding figure hanging on the garden fence certainly was an impressive scarecrow. With an enormous straw hat. A threatening totem to keep all manner of predators away from the delicate vegetables.

Didi began to climb the three-step porch.

"Wait a minute, Miss!"

It was Charlie who had shouted.

"Wait for what?" Didi asked.

"That ain't no scarecrow."

Didi blinked the sun out of her eyes. She began to run toward the behatted object. Then she turned away, quickly, violently.

Charlie was right. It wasn't a scarecrow. That was Mary Hyndman hanging on the fence. And there were three small holes in the center of her forehead. Neat, well-placed bullet holes.

Chapter 2

Didi drank the vodka down, fast and straight. She gagged on it. Her eyes burned.

"You better go easy on that, Miss," she heard a voice in her ear.

She turned angrily toward the voice. It was Charlie Gravis. "Are you following me around, Charlie?" she demanded.

"No, Miss. We just seem to always be at the same place."

"Why don't you help Mrs. Tunney get some more food out?"

"Will do, Miss," Charlie agreed. But he didn't move.

The party swirled around her. Didi knew all the people—merchants, dairy farmers, old friends of her mother, neighbors. She had invited them all to her birthday party because she wanted to thank them for their friendship and help.

But standing there, she felt some very odd feelings. That this wasn't her mother's house . . . that these people were in the wrong house . . . that it wasn't really her birthday.

I must not have any more of this poison, she thought, crushing the paper cup.

A woman with a fat, florid face grabbed her and kissed her.

"Mrs. Grange's daughter," said Charlie in her ear after the woman had moved on.

Didi stared at Charlie Gravis for a moment and then looked away. She remembered that it was Charlie who had discovered the body. She had thought it was a scarecrow. How long ago was that? Not more than three hours. And other than Charlie and herself, not a soul in the house knew that Mary Hyndman had been murdered.

The Hillsbrook police had come quickly. And then the state troopers. But there was little to tell them. Detective Allie Voegler pressed Charlie and Didi for information on the license plate of the physician's vehicle. But neither of them could recall a single number. All they could agree on was that Dr. Purdy from Dover Plains was driving a green station wagon with MD plates. As for the model and make of the station wagon, Charlie thought it was a Ford Taurus wagon, while Didi thought it was an imported car—a Mitsubishi perhaps.

"Isn't it crazy, Charlie?" she asked him suddenly.

"What?"

"That no one at the party except you and I knows that Mary Hyndman was murdered."

"Maybe we ought to tell them, Miss."

"Well, that's going to be nice and festive, isn't it? Who's going to stand up and make the announcement—you or me?"

Charlie Gravis didn't answer. He had finally picked up on the fact that Didi Quinn Nightingale had had too much vodka—too much and too quickly. He went and got her a cup of coffee and a chair. Didi sat down and sipped carefully from the paper cup. Charlie stood over her, a sort of geriatric bodyguard.

Then Mrs. Tunney passed by, noticed Didi's condition, and swiftly ordered her to eat a small slab of soft, sharp New York State cheddar on a salted cracker. Then came another cup of coffee. Presently Didi was sober again. Depressed, but sober.

"You look better, Miss," Charlie said.

"Do I?" she wonderd out loud.

She began to search the room worriedly, trying to spot her friend Rose Vigdor, whom she had invited to the party at least a dozen times. There was no sign of her in the crowd.

"Charlie, have you see Rose?"

He made a scornful face and shrugged; as if finding Rose was far from top priority.

Charlie's reaction infuriated Didi. She had no patience for his view of new residents in Hillsbrook—namely, that they were extraterrestrials. Oh, not that they should be persecuted or anything; just simply avoided at all times.

Two children ran past. Boys. They were wearing turned-around baseball caps. Didi had no idea who they were. She had the sudden revelation that they were really goats from a nearby milking herd. Everybody knew that goats were magical creatures who could transform themselves into other life forms—little boys, old ladies, anything.

She smiled. Her mother had told her that

when she was a child. But Didi had no idea where her mother had picked up that very fanciful old wives' tale.

She remembered something else her mother had told her: "No one who puts his hands to the plow and looks back is fit for the Kingdom of God."

It was from the Gospel of Luke. Didi had never understood what it meant and her mother had never bothered to explain.

She burst into tears at the memory. Then stood up quickly and turned away from Charlie Gravis . . . right into a grinning Trent Tucker, who said: "Allie Voegler is around front, in his police car. He wants to talk to you and Charlie." Young Trent always found the strangest things amusing.

"Didn't you invite him to the party?" Charlie Gravis asked as they both headed toward the door.

"Of course I did. But he has a murder on his hands. Or don't you remember, Charlie?"

The old man grumbled. They walked out of the house and approached the car.

Suddenly two of the yard dogs appeared from nowhere and leaped up against Didi, begging her to play. Charlie was too slow to stop them and Didi never saw them coming.

She yelled at them and pushed them away, but it was too late for her now mud-spattered party dress.

She looked quickly at Allie Voegler behind the wheel. He was trying to keep a straight face. Yes, she thought, he *would* get a kick out of this. He liked anything that got her muddy, bruised her ego, embarrassed her, took her down a peg. He was convinced that she was a social climber and the reason she wouldn't sleep with him—let alone marry him—was that he was a lowly village plainclothes cop and she a veterinarian to the rich and famous. Of course Didi knew that was unmitigated nonsense. Her clients were neither rich nor famous; most of them were about a dollar short of bankruptcy, and often a day ahead of the sheriff. As for her class bias—that, too, was bunk. There were undeniably many reasons she and Allie had not become lovers, but money and status weren't among them. There was simply a powerful attraction, and equally powerful repulsion at work between them. Just one of those things. Inexplicable.

"It could have been worse," Charlie said, making a valiant effort to remove some of the mud with his handkerchief. Didi shook off the help.

When they reached the unmarked police car, Allie leaned out the window and said: "Maybe you and Charlie started drinking early today."

"What are you talking about?" she demanded angrily.

"Well, it turns out that your friend in the green station wagon doesn't exist," replied a laconic Allie Voegler, shifting his large frame in the front seat for emphasis. "There is no Dr. Purdy practicing or living in Dover Plains. And the County Medical Society said there is no Purdy practicing in Dutchess County. There is one in Schoherie County, but he's skinny and bald and drives a Lexus."

"I saw what I saw!" Charlie protested.

Didi was too astonished to say anything.

Allie Voegler continued: "Also, Dr. Fisk wasn't on vacation. And his office received no call from Mary Hyndman. She did call about a week ago to tell Dr. Fisk she was doing fine."

"Did you find a puppy?" Didi asked.

"No puppy. And we looked hard. In the house . . . in her garden . . . in the woods. Nothing. We did find a feeding bowl and some rubber bones and some boxes of Puppy Chow. We also found some signs a dog had marked the sides of her house. But no puppy."

There was silence.

"You people have nothing to say?" Allie pushed.

Didi retorted angrily. "Are you also going to tell us that it wasn't Mary Hyndman hanging on that fence with three bullet holes in her face?"

"No. You got that part right," he said. Allie Voegler turned the engine over and started to pull away. Then he put the brakes on hard and stuck his head out the window. "I almost forgot, Didi." He reached into the backseat, picked something up and shoved it through the window toward her. "Your birthday gift."

Didi reluctantly took it and found herself staring at a brand-new, outsize baseball bat.

"I figured," Allie said, "that a beautiful young veterinarian like Didi Nightingale needs something to keep four-legged suitors away. Maybe even two-legged ones."

Allie drove off, sending mud onto Charlie's and Didi's shoes.

Didi turned the bat over in her hands as if she were examining it. But her thoughts were on that red-haired man in the green station wagon and the scarecrow he had left on the fence.

"Don't you think you should get back to your party, Miss?" Charlie suggested. "Folks are gonna think—"

"In a minute, Charlie. In a minute."

Chapter 3

Didi assumed the lotus position on the ground in the yard behind the big stone house. It was 6 A.M.

To her left was the old barn that now housed only the pigs, which her retainers raised in spite of her objections. Directly in front of her and extending several hundred yards was the old alfalfa field, now untilled. Past the field was the small pond and then the magnificent stand of white pine that had been her mother's pride and joy.

It was a beautiful morning on the cusp of deep summer—a little bit of chill, a little bit of heat.

Didi began her breathing exercises. She practiced a rudimentary form of Pranayama— a form of Yoga that concentrates on regulating the inhalation and expiration of the breath.

Just as she was about to hold her first measured inhalation, she saw a spot of white flash across the field. It was a doe and her fawn, drinking at the pond.

She loved watching the deer drink. They were so careful. One quick dip of their lovely necks into the water, and then the almost

panicky survey of the land, looking for ene-
mies. Drink and look. Drink and look. Always
wary. Of course, outside of hunting season,
they had nothing to fear expect the rare pack
of stray dogs.

The fawn was very young, still with a hint
of wobble. Didi smiled. She had assisted in a
great many births the past three months. It
was that time of year: mares dropping foals,
cows dropping calves, does dropping kids,
ewes dropping lambs.

The smile vanished. Spring and early summer always brought professional and financial
rewards to vets. You made it then, or you
didn't make it at all. The problem was, as Hillsbrook became increasingly suburbanized,
Didi had to travel farther and farther to outly-
ing dairy and horse farms. Sometimes four
hours of travel time, for one client. That was
not good. Of course her small animal practice
was booming, but her heart was with the cows
and horses.

Didi straightened her back with a jolt, angry
at herself for having become distracted. She
had learned the "Yoga of Breathing" from a
woman in Philadelphia while she was at vet
school. And her "guru" had always said, "If
you want to harness the vital force you must
do it quickly and with great concentration."

She resumed the exercises. When she was
finished she rose, stretched, and looked into
the kitchen window.

No one was up yet. Usually her "elves," as
she called the nonpaying boarders she had inherited from her mother, were having break-

fast when she finished her exercises. But she couldn't fault them this morning. Her birthday party had run later than expected and there had been a lot to clean up. Besides, Didi hadn't helped at all. In fact, she might as well not have shown up to her own party, because she was inebriated during it. Her mother would have been mortified. But then again, her mother had always said that when she was good, she was very good and when she was bad . . .

Even her mother would have excused Didi's excesses of last night, though. But, thankfully, her mother had not lived to see Mary Hyndman a murder victim.

Didi heard the car pulling up in the front of the house. She hesitated only a second, brushed off the seat of her jeans, and headed toward the visitor. When people pulled up to her place at this hour it usually meant they had hit a deer on the road and they wanted Didi to clean up the mess.

But the visitor wasn't reporting a road kill.

It was Harold Tepper, the pharmacist in Hillsbrook. He stayed in his old, well-kept car as Didi approached.

"Good morning, Dr. Nightingale," he said.

"Good morning, Mr. Tepper," she replied.

He was a very formal man. He had owned and run the small pharmacy on Main Street for twenty-nine years. Everyone knew it was going under now because people went to the drug chains in the malls. But Mr. Tepper never complained.

"It is a terrible thing what happened to Mary Hyndman," he said.

"Yes, horrible," Didi agreed.

"Did you see the morning paper yet?"

"No."

"Well, it said that Mary Hyndman was shot to death by a .22-caliber long handgun. And the killer may have been a man seen leaving the Hyndman place, passing as a physician." He paused, pushed his eyeglasses up, and leaned further out the window.

"The paper also says, Dr. Nightingale, that you and Charlie Gravis were at the scene and spoke to the man."

"Yes, we did," Didi affirmed. She turned back toward the house, where three of the yard dogs and one cat had started an early-morning altercation, mainly to attract the attention of Abigail, the pretty young "elf" who customarily fed them. But Abigail was going to feed herself first.

"Quiet! All of you!" Didi barked back at them. Then she turned back to Mr. Tepper. "We found her body hanging on a fence, like a scarecrow."

"Terrible, Dr. Nightingale."

"It couldn't be worse, Mr. Tepper."

There was a long, awkward silence. Didi had no idea why Mr. Tepper had come by. Particularly at this hour of the morning. Mr. Tepper was not known for this sociability.

He squirmed in the driver's seat, took off his glasses, put them back on and finally said, "You know, poor Mary was financially strapped. Everyone thought she had money, but she didn't have a dime."

"Yes. I figured that. She never paid me for putting down her Shepherd bitch, and I never pressed her."

"She couldn't even pay for her medicine. Did you know that?"

Didi didn't know what to say.

"So I gave it to her anyway."

"That was nice of you, Mr. Tepper."

"What else could I do? She was a wonderful old lady."

"Yes, she was."

He heaved a large sigh for such a little man, and added: "She asked me to do her a favor if she died, Dr. Nightingale. And that's why I'm here."

He pulled out of the car's glove compartment an old sock of black wool, knotted at the top. It was the type of black wool sock proper women used to wear—ugly and scratchy.

He handed it through the open window to Didi.

"She saved a little bit of money in the sock. She left it with me. In case of her death, she told me, I was to bring it to you, and you were to take it to the monks of Alsatian House. As a gift to them in her memory."

Didi opened the knot. She reached into the sock and pulled out a batch of crumpled bills. A few twenties, a few tens, a few ones. Maybe a hundred dollars at most—if that. How sad!

"Do you know them?" he asked.

"You mean the monks? Alsatian House? I know of them. It's a monastery in Columbia

County, on the Hudson. They're famous for breeding German shepherd dogs."

"Then you'll get the money to them?"

"Of course. I drive up to a thoroughbred farm in Columbia County about twice a month. I'll bring it to them the next time I go up."

"I thank you, Dr. Nightingale. It's the least we can do for Mary Hyndman."

And off he drove. Didi walked back to the house, entered through the front door, and headed up the staircase to her bedroom.

Halfway up she stopped. She stared at the sock. What was the matter with her? Why was she postponing a trip to the monks? This was Mary Hyndman's last wish. It would be unkind to wait. Why shouldn't she bring the money to the Alsatian House now and let the dead rest in peace?

Didi turned, walked down the stairs and headed toward the kitchen to see if Charlie Gravis was awake. She would tell him to get ready for the trip to the monastery.

Yes, Charlie was up. All the elves were. Charlie, Trent Tucker, and Abigail were seated at the long kitchen table waiting for Mrs. Tunney to finish the oatmeal.

Didi hesitated before entering the kitchen proper. Why did Mrs. Tunney cook oatmeal twelve months of the year? Why did the others eat it twelve months of the year? Didi loathed oatmeal but she was always fascinated by the sight of Mrs. Tunney and her enormous pot. Morning after morning, unto eternity.

Trent Tucker and Charlie were waiting, as

usual, side by side, spoons gripped. Mrs. Tunney always served Charlie first, then Trent, then Abigail.

Didi smiled as she looked at the wraithlike Abigail . . . so pale, so quiet, so ethereal. Everybody said she had screws loose, but Didi didn't believe that. The young woman was just strange. Many musical people were like that and Abigail was definitely musical. In fact, she had studied two years in a conservatory in Rochester.

Didi stopped just short of the kitchen doorway, stopped herself from calling out to Charlie. Good heavens, why hadn't she thought of it sooner? There was someone who'd make a much more amiable companion on the drive to Alsatian House.

Why don't I take Rose Vigdor along with me? Didi suddenly thought.

Rose loved dogs, and particularly German Shepherds. After all, she had one: a lovely spayed Shepherd bitch named Aretha. Rose's other dog was a male Corgi named Huck.

Without a word, Didi walked out of the house, climbed into her red jeep and drove a mile down the road to the three-acre homestead of her friend Rose Vigdor.

She smiled as she pulled the car up in front of the enormous, still half-finished cow barn that functioned as Rose's domicile.

Didi could hear the carpentry being done inside. Rose always woke in the small hours of the morning to get an early start on the day. Winter and summer there was wood to be measured and cut, because Rose had decided to refurbish the ancient barn all by herself. But eight months after moving to Hillsbrook she had hardly made a dent. The roof of the barn was a patchwork of old and new lumber with many holes still remaining, covered by canvas and waterproof tarps.

There was no doubt that many natives of Hillsbrook, Charlie Gravis included, considered Rose Vigdor quite eccentric. She was one of the long line of city dwellers who had moved to Hillsbrook to "become one with nature." There were organic farmers and mystics and breeders of exotic animals—a whole host of latter-day Thoreaus who had purchased land in this part of Dutchess County.

But Rose was something special. She had refused to run power lines onto her property. There was no electricity. She cooked on a wood-burning potbellied stove. She used candles. And she had refused to put in plumbing. There was an outhouse just behind the barn—a well-appointed one, but an outhouse nevertheless. And there was absolutely no running water in the barn; she had simply resuscitated an old well.

Rose Vigdor was a young woman, not yet thirty, and had worked for almost nine years at a record company in Manhattan. Then she had taken all her savings and fled to Nature.

Didi had made her acquaintance during the winter when she had treated one of Rose's dogs for an eye infection. And they had quickly become friends. Didi loved to sit in the huge barn and listen to Rose's absurdly overoptimistic plans for the future. After she finished the barn, Rose would say, she was going to raise llamas and grow esoteric fruit trees. Or she was going to breed Sicilian donkeys and create a new breed of organic radish. Her imagination was fertile. And Didi found her stories about life in the fast lane of the music business equally fascinating.

The moment Didi stepped out of the jeep the two dogs barreled through the slightly open barn door and leaped on her. Two seconds later they had become so entangled in each other—being one was short and one was high—they began a mock battle and forgot about Didi.

Rose was at her usual place—in front of the worktable, surrounded by tools, planks, and how-to manuals. She was wearing her carpenter's jeans, the ones with two hundred pockets. Her blond hair was straight, not long, and she had bangs. Rose Vigdor was a large woman, not fat, just big. And her face was blunt, but almost pixieish. She wore canvas boating sneakers so she could keep her grip on the many ladders she was always scaling.

The moment Rose saw Didi she raised her hands in a gesture of surrender. "You're right, Didi, I'm guilty! Guilty, guilty, guilty! I tried to make it to your party, but I just couldn't get things under control here. I'm a miserable no-account creature. I'm no friend to anyone."

Didi laughed. "It's okay. I forgive you."

Rose put her hands down.

"Anyway," Didi added, "you didn't miss much. The party was a bust."

"Why?"

"Didn't you hear about the murder?"

"The what!"

"Yes. Mary Hyndman was murdered on the morning of the party. Charlie and I went to pick her up, to bring her back here to the party. We found her body."

"Who is Mary Hyndman?"

"And old woman. She lived in Hillsbrook all her life."

"I thought you people up here didn't kill each other."

"You thought wrong," Didi said. "Anyway, Rose, the reason I barged in so early is that I thought you might like to take a ride with me up to Columbia County."

"When?"

"Today. In about an hour."

"What for? I mean, where are you going? Or is it just, you know, like, a . . . ride?"

"I'm going up to Alsatian House."

Rose's eyes opened wider. "Ah, Didi. You mean to the German shepherd monastery."

"Correct."

Rose laughed. "But I already have a German shepherd." She called out to Aretha, who glided in to get her ears scratched. Then Rose said to Didi: "I didn't know you were looking for a house dog."

"I'm not. I have no interest at this time in buying a puppy."

"Didi, you can't *buy* a dog there anyway."

"Of course you can, if you want to. They sell German shepherds, just like some monasteries make and sell cheese or wine or jams."

"No. No! No!" Rose corrected her. "I read all

about Alsatian House. They don't *sell* their dogs. They literally give them away to deserving people. Once you get one, you can make a donation if you want . . . but they don't sell them."

"You're probably right, Rose. I don't know anything about them except that their dogs are supposed to be wonderful."

In a voice of mock betrayal she asked, "Are you saying, Dr. Nightingale, that those monks have dogs more wonderful than Aretha and Huck? Are you saying that?" She dropped the joke voice then and said reflectively: "You know, I read about those dogs. People talk about them. But no one ever says what is so special about them. Well, let me know. I'm sorry, Didi, but I want to keep working. I'm on a roll here."

Didi stared up at the cavernous unfinished roof and rolled her eyes.

"It's getting there, Didi!" Rose said. "Have faith!"

"See ya when I get back," Didi said, and walked out to her jeep.

Rose followed her to her car. "Wait, Didi. I want to ask you a personal question."

"What?"

"I hope you won't be insulted."

"Veterinarians have very thick skin, Rose."

"Okay. What is going on with those people in your house?"

"What people?"

"You know, the ones you . . . live with. I mean, are they tenants, or what?"

"Oh," Didi said, suddenly understanding

what Rose meant, "you mean you want to know the secret history of my elves."

"Why do you call them elves?"

"I don't know. What else should I call them? They were willed to me by my mother."

"Do they work only for you?"

"Why, Rose? Do you want to hire Mrs. Tunney to make you oatmeal each morning? Believe me, she won't work on a potbellied stove."

"No, no oatmeal. But I want to hire that young man, Trent Somebody or Other."

"For what?"

"To haul all the garbage on my land to the town dump."

"Well, sure. He hires out his pickup truck from time to time. He doesn't tell me about it, but he does. I don't stop them from earning outside money as long as they earn their keep doing what they're supposed to do around my property."

"Do I call your number and ask for him?"

"Relax, Rose. I'll leave a note for him before I go to Columbia County. I'll tell him to stop by and see you."

"Thanks. Oh, there's one other question—What kind of wages should I pay him?"

"Let your conscience be your guide," Didi said, closing the door of the jeep. She started the engine and headed back home.

Halfway there she thought of another travelmate who would surely make better company than the grumpy old Charlie Gravis. She might as well take Abigail, who would surely enjoy the dog-breeding monks more than Charlie would, and maybe almost as much as Rose would have.

Chapter 4

"Listen, Joe, do you know why when they decided to use a plainclothes cop in Hillsbrook they selected me?"

Joe Creed, the bartender at Roadhouse 44, just outside Hillsbrook on Route 44, shook his head.

"No, Allie. I haven't the faintest idea."

"Because I don't look like a cop, Joe. I look like a dairy farmer. I'm big, rangy, and quiet. That's why."

"Well, Allie, there aren't enough dairy farmers left around Hillsbrook for it to matter."

Allie, who usually drank only beer this early, swallowed what was left of his Jack Daniel's.

"It should matter to Didi. She thinks dairy farmers can walk on water," he said bitterly.

"Didi who?" the bartender asked.

Allie straightened his frame and ran one hand through his thick, longish hair.

"I'm talking about Deirdre Quinn Nightingale, DVM. Or is it MVD?"

"People say she's a helluva vet," Joe Creed said.

Allie leaned over the bar, taking Joe Creed into his confidence. "Listen, that woman not only breaks my heart but she makes me do stupid things."

"What kind of stupid things?"

"I gave her a baseball bat for her birthday."

"Why?"

"I don't know. I told you, she makes me do stupid things."

"Relax, Allie. I once gave my wife a pair of red long johns."

Allie didn't reply. The connection was vague to him. He turned and stared out the windows onto the highway. He was off duty but he couldn't relax. And the alcohol wasn't helping.

"I need a cup of coffee," he said.

"Sure," Joe Creed agreed. He walked to the other end of the bar where an urn was set up, drew a mug, and walked it back to Allie.

He took a long swallow and grimaced. Their coffee was always terrible. He twirled the mug between his palms. He thought of Didi again. But this time in a professional vein. Why couldn't she have identified some numbers on that bogus doctor's license plate? Just two would have been enough. Just two.

It was just past noon when the red jeep carrying Didi and Abigail arrived at the monastery in Northwestern Columbia County.

The parking lot was isolated and bordered by runaway berry bushes. They left the car and followed the only path out of the lot. They could not see the Hudson, but they could see the enormous Saratoga-type house on a perfectly landscaped lawn. It seemed to be three stories high, with hundreds of windows, and a high wraparound porch. The house was built out of wood and newly painted blue. The shape was of an inverted horseshoe—the two wings moving inland away from the river.

"There aren't too many of these kinds of houses left," Didi commented to Abigail. Then she added wryly: "When the Hudson was owned by the rich."

Abigail did not respond; nor was Didi expecting her to. The trip up there had been delightful. It was the first long trip she had ever taken alone with Abigail and the strange young woman's silence had been oddly comforting.

As they approached the house from the south side, Didi caught a glimpse of the slope behind one of the wings—cultivated fields and low-lying sheds.

Suddenly Didi felt Abigail's arm on hers.

She turned and saw that a man was standing not more than twenty feet away from them.

"Welcome," he called out. He was pushing a wheelbarrow full of horse manure, festooned with wisps of hay.

He moved closer and dropped the handles of the wheelbarrow. He was a tall, thin, hawklike man, wearing a tattered sweatshirt, patched chinos, and mismatched sandals. His face and clothing were stained with sweat and grime.

"Can you tell me where the—" Didi stopped in the middle of her sentence. She really didn't know who she was looking for. Who was the head of this monastery? What was his title?

Then she remembered a title. "Can you direct me to the abbot?"

"My name is Brother Neil," the man said, "and we don't have an abbot. But you must mean Brother Thomas. Just walk into the house, turn right and follow the hallway to his office. You can wait for him there. I will fetch him." He flashed a very broad smile, picked up his wheelbarrow, and moved off.

Didi and Abigail walked up the steps and opened the door. They followed the hallway, came to another door, opened it and stepped inside, closing it gently behind them.

Yes, it was a sort of office. But the furnishings were bizarre, nothing even remotely resembled order. It was obvious that the chairs and tables, even the desk and the lamps had been rescued from the dump heaps and then revived to the best of the monk's abilities.

Didi sat down in a frayed armchair. Abigail sat on a rickety dining-room chair. There were several doors in and out of the office and the windows were huge and open.

"Did you ever see such empty walls?" Didi asked. "I mean, there are no crosses, no religious pictures, no symbols of any kind. What kind of monastery is it?"

Abigail looked around but didn't answer. Didi studied the huge rattan desk, one end piled high with papers. She imagined a grizzled old scholar sitting there, poring over ancient texts late into the tropical night, at his elbow a long-necked bottle of the liquor that had ruined his life.

Suddenly two shapes exploded through an open window. Didi instinctively threw her arms across her face, to protect herself.

Two German shepherd dogs had leaped through the open window into the office. They stood there calmly, their tongues lolling, inspecting the strangers.

So these were the famous "monk dogs." Her fear gone, Didi studied them. Yes, they were magnificent creatures—both males, both less than a year old.

But they were the old-style shepherds. Their backs were straight and not sloped like the progeny of American breeders who had achieved sloping backs and thereby doomed the breed to hip disorders. And they were not as long as their American counterparts and their coats were thicker and less flashy. The snout, too, was shorter, and the ears wider and just slightly, ever so slightly, tufted.

One of them groaned and flopped down onto the floor.

The other one casually climbed onto a startled Abigail's lap. It was a lapful, indeed.

Abigail laughed . . . a brilliant, almost singsong laugh that seemed to bounce against the walls of the strange office. It was the first time Didi had ever heard the young woman laugh.

Then a door opened and an old man walked in. He was small and thin with close-cropped white hair. His skin was translucent and he walked slowly but easily. Like Abigail herself, he gave the impression of floating rather than walking through the world.

"I am Brother Thomas. You wish to see me?"

Didi stood up. "My name is Deirdre Quinn Nightingale and this is my assistant, Abigail. I'm a veterinarian from Hillsbrook."

"Ah," he said, "in Dutchess County."

Didi nodded.

Brother Thomas, who was wearing an old woolen vest over a polo shirt, pointed at the dog on Abigail's lap. "That is Horatio." Then he pointed to the dog on the floor. "That is Jack."

"They are magnificent," Didi said.

Brother Thomas smiled, walked behind his desk, and sat down. The dogs moaned, as if understanding that business was about to be transacted, and flew out the window. Abigail looked very sad as the parcel departed from her lap.

Didi reached into her shoulder bag and pulled out the sock. She unknotted it, removed the crumpled money, and took it over to the desk. She smoothed and counted the bills quickly. "A neighbor of mine died, Brother Thomas. She had saved this money and her last wish was that I deliver it personally to you."

Brother Thomas smiled.

"It is only a hundred and nineteen dollars, but she was a poor woman at the end."

"Thank you very much. All contributions are needed. Your friend has been good to us. I am sure she was blessed."

Didi was about to blurt out that she had not been blessed; on the contrary, she had been savagely murdered. But she held back.

Brother Thomas folded the money, fastened it with a rubber band, and laid it on top of the pile of papers.

"I'm curious," Didi said. "Are you a Catholic monastery? Or Episcopalian?"

"We have Catholics here. And Protestants. And Jews and Buddhists and atheists. We're not a monastery in the ordinary sense. The brothers and sisters worship whom they wish to worship. Our goal is simply to live together—humans and dogs—in the Spirit. And thereby to increase the love in the world. That is all we do."

His words made her uncomfortable but they intrigued her. "What Spirit do you mean?" she asked.

He smiled and shrugged, then replied: "You have come a long way to deliver your gift. Let me show you about. And then please grace our meal with your presence."

Didi accepted with a nod. What was the rush? And she was curious.

Brother Thomas led the two women out of the office and down one wing of the horseshoe. It was the monks' quarters ... a series of small rooms, each one identically furnished with a cot, a chair, and a chest, nothing more. The bathrooms were communal—men on one side, women on the other.

Then he walked them to the opposite wing. "This is for our visitors, from the outside. It is a little more opulent. Many people come here on retreats in the fall and winter. They pay a small daily fee that we use to survive."

Didi jumped as something cold and wet went into her palm. She looked down. It was another dog. A magnificent mature German shepherd bitch with a blackish face. Didi laughed and knelt down. "Well, who are you, my fine lady?"

"That is Veronica," said Brother Thomas.

Didi pulled ever so gently on Veronica's left ear. "I see," she said, "that you don't keep the dogs in the kennels."

"We don't have kennels," replied Brother Thomas.

Then he added: "When we have to isolate a bitch in heat we just keep her in one of the vistors' rooms."

Didi stood up. This was a very strange place . . . a dog-breeding operation without kennels.

"But where do the dogs sleep?" she asked.

"Wherever they wish," Brother Thomas replied.

They walked down the vistors' wing, followed by Veronica. As in the rest of the house, the walls were bare.

"And here is where we pray and sing," Brother Thomas announced, opening a door. Didi peered in. There were several chairs and benches and stools scattered about in no discernible pattern. And a piano.

"The chapel?"

"We don't call it a chapel, but you may call it that. Those who want to, assemble each morning about six. Whoever wishes can speak or sing."

Speak about what? Sing what? Didi thought. And Brother Thomas picked up on her bewilderment.

"Sometimes a gospel passage is spoken about. This morning, I believe, Brother Lawrence spoke about that passage from John: *My food is to do the will of Him who sent me.* And, if I recall, the day before, Sister Pia spoke about *the thoughtful elation that has no end.* A T'ang poem. Eighth century. Chinese. As for singing—well, we do whatever the Spirit demands."

The Spirit again, Didi thought. This old, quite lovely man, keeps mentioning the Spirit, but he doesn't define it. She was a veterinarian. She was a scientist. She had no quarrel with any kind of religious faith, but there had to be some kind of precision in language. Then she caught herself—and felt foolish. Why was she getting so involved with this old man's language? Or beliefs?

They walked out onto the back porch. Didi breathed deeply. Laid out before their eyes was a lovely sight. Small cultivated fields with narrow borders between them, gently sloping away. Men and women were working in the fields. Several German shepherds were playing in the borders.

"If you pardon my arrogance, we are almost self-sufficient. In food, that is," Brother Thomas said. "We grow squash and beans and tomatoes and rye and potatoes." He pointed to a shed in the distance. "And we used to raise our own chickens there."

"Why did you stop?"

"Newcastle disease."

"Did you lose the whole flock?" Didi asked, knowing that the viral disease called RMV-1 could be horrific. In 1984 a plague of RMV-1 decimated the U.S. poultry industry.

"Yes. It was terrible. First they couldn't breathe. Then they couldn't eat. Then they began to circle and tremble. And then they died. Now a local farmer brings us eggs and dressed chickens and turkeys."

At that moment Veronica decided to leave the group and she bounded off in that beautiful shepherd gait. The sun caught her coat. This was the third of the monk dogs that Didi has seen up close and they all had wonderful coats . . . healthy, thick, burnished. It was easy to see why their dogs were so sought after.

"Do you see that building there?" Brother Thomas asked, pointing to what looked like a long tent. Both sides of the tent were rolled up and the poles were buttressed by cinder blocks.

"That is where we eat," he explained. "I must do some last-minute chores, so I will leave both of you now. But please join us for the meal. It should be ready just about now."

Didi stared at her watch. It was one o'clock. If they left now they wouldn't be back in Hillsbrook until around three. She had nothing on her calendar, but something may have come up.

"We really must be getting back, Brother Thomas," Didi said apologetically.

Then she saw the look of sadness suddenly crease Abigail's face. It was obvious she wanted to stay very much. Well, why not eat before they left? Otherwise they would have to stop off on the road.

"On second thought, we would be delighted to eat with you," Didi amended. And she knew immediately that she had made absolutely the right decision.

*   *   *

Allie Voegler called in from Roadhouse 44. He discovered that the coroner's report had confirmed what they already knew about the death of Mary Hyndman; that the state police had done a thorough search of the premises and found nothing; that all of Mary Hyndman's possessions in her house seemed to be intact; that no progress had been made in identifying or locating the bogus doctor who was the only suspect they had.

Allie went back to the bar, drank his third cup of coffee, finished his grilled cheese and bacon sandwich, and stared at himself in the bar mirror until he determined that he was thoroughly sober. Then he went out to his car and drove to Mary Hyndman's place.

A Hillsbrook police cruiser was parked in front. On the porch of the house stood a uniformed officer; it was the new man, Wynton Chung.

Allie parked his vehicle haphazardly and walked to the house. He didn't care that the state police had made a thorough search; he was going to find that goddamn puppy, if indeed there was a puppy. But if there hadn't been a puppy, why the Puppy Chow and the rubber bones? And why would the suspect have mentioned it to Didi?

"What's up?" Allie asked Wynton Chung.

"Nothing much, Allie. I was told to secure the premises," replied rookie Chung. He was the first nonwhite in the history of the Hillsbrook Police Department. Chung's father was Chinese and his mother black. He was born

and raised in Kingston, New York, and went
to the State University at New Paltz. In fact,
he was also the first college graduate in the
history of the department. Chung had been on
the force for three months and he was not
popular. Not at all. He was stiff, hard to know,
guarded. Everything was a problem, everything a threat.

Allie, though, liked him. Mostly because he
was a different color; Allie was weary of white
faces forever.

"You here on business?" Chung queried.

Allie raised his eyebrows. "No. Pleasure," he
retorted, and Chung laughed. "I'm looking for
that goddamn puppy."

"Yeah, I heard about that ghost puppy."

"You sure it's a ghost?" Allie asked.

"The way I figure it is this: Suppose there
was a puppy. His mistress is cut down by gun-
shots. The puppy is going to run like hell into
the woods and hide. He'd be scared out of his
skin. But sooner or later the puppy is going to
come back where there is food and water. With
a puppy, I'd say sooner rather than later.
Right?"

"You're probably right, Wynton. Probably
right. But I like looking for lost puppies. Hell,
before all those rich lunatics moved into the
Hillsbrook areas with all their drug treatment
programs and ashrams and organic farms . . .
that's all Hillsbrook cops did, clean up after
road kills and look for lost puppies."

"Have a good time," Wynton Chung said.

Allie surveyed the terrain. He remembered
how K-9 dogs and their handlers search for a

missing child. Identify the last place seen. Then use that place as a center and continue outward in larger and larger circles always keeping that place as the center of the circle.

Assuming the elusive puppy really existed, the house had to be the last place it was seen. So, Allie made a circle of the house and then a larger circle and a larger one. Soon, he was slogging through brush and forest and over-grown gardens.

It had not started out as a particularly warm day, but the sun's intensity had been steadily building. The mounting heat, along with his early drinking, had begun to take its toll. He moved more and more slowly. He discovered nothing other than the droppings that could have been left by any number of wandering or wild dogs. Once in a while he sang out a desultory whistle, or called "Here, boy! Here, pup!"—hoping to draw a response—but the only answer came from the mischievous, tree-hopping blackbirds overhead.

Finally, disgusted, Allie headed back to the house. He joined Wynton Chung inside. Chung was seated on the old sofa reading a magazine. His weapon, in its holster, a brand new Glock 9mm, was on the small table in front of him.

"Any luck?"

"Nothing. Is there anything in the frig?"

"Haven't looked."

Allie walked into the kitchen and opened the refrigerator door. No juice, no soda, no beer. Just half an apple, some eggs, a small piece of cheddar cheese, and one head of lettuce wrapped in cellophane. On one of the refrigerator door shelves was an almost empty bottle of commercial salad dressing.

He closed the door and opened the top, the freezer door. Inside were six packages wrapped in aluminum foil.

He opened the top one—a thick-cut pork chop. He opened the second one—another pork chop. A third try revealed a third chop. He slammed the freezer door shut and rejoined Chung.

"Nothing?"

"Not a thing."

"Then just let the water run."

"I'm leaving now anyway. I'll stop off at the general store."

He headed toward the door but then hesitated. There was something very peculiar about an old woman having an empty refrigerator and a freezer full of pork chops. It just bothered him. He turned and walked swiftly back into the kitchen, opened the freezer door and once again unwrapped the top pork chop. He studied it. It certainly wasn't store bought: it was much too thick and the fat on the edges hadn't been trimmed at all. Now, that *was* strange.

Chapter 5

Didi and Abigail stood just inside the large tent where lunch was being served. It reminded Didi of the mess tent she had seen on the reruns of the television series *M*A*S*H*. A line of servers doled out the food to people with trays, who then brought their trays to tables to eat.

"Look, there's Brother Thomas," Didi said, spotting the old man on the line, tray in hand.

Abigail moved toward the line. Didi's hand on Abigail's shoulder stayed her. "Will you look at that!" she exclaimed quietly. "Can you believe that, Abigail?"

Interspersed with the people on the line, the brothers and sisters, were the German shepherds.

They were actually waiting on line, waiting to be served their lunch!

And each of them held in his jaws, calmly, a long-handled bowl.

The servers filled the dogs' bowls with the exact same food they were spooning onto the trays of the monastery residents.

Didi laughed quietly and nervously. She just had never seen anything like this. Oh, everyone knows a pooch who, upon hearing a dog food can being opened, picks up his bowl and heads toward the sound. It does not require a great deal of canine intelligence. But the idea of dogs waiting calmly on the same food line as people was just outside Didi's experience— even if the dogs involved were the notoriously intelligent German shepherds.

She watched the line, waiting for mayhem to erupt. It didn't. Once the dogs' bowls were filled they carried them to the perimeter of the tent, flopped down and began eating.

"Well," Didi said to Abigail, "at least they're not using the tables and chairs."

Didi and Abigail joined the line. Their trays were heaped with assorted savory vegetables, chicken cutlets, fruit, and rice. The food smelled delicious.

They headed toward the table where Brother Thomas was seated.

On the way they were hailed by one of the brothers who called out "Welcome! Again!"

It was the hawklike man whom they had met on the lawn . . . the man with the wheelbarrow full of manure who had introduced himself as Brother Neil.

They waved to him but continued the journey to Brother Thomas's table. Didi noticed that the look this Brother Neil gave Abigail was more than hospitality. It seemed like old-fashioned lust.

"Please, join me," Brother Thomas said. They slid into their seats across from him.

"Are the people who live here celibate, Brother Thomas?"

The old man was not shocked at all by Didi's question. He chewed carefully until he swallowed. Then he said: "You know, Dr. Nightingale, a very wise man once said: Do not cultivate a bogus or an imitative religiosity, because the path from the monastery to the tavern is very short."

Didi laughed. "Brother Thomas, I was talking about sex, not booze."

"Well, yes, you were. But the truth is the same. No, we have no rules enforcing celibacy here. But yes, all those who live here are celibate. Because they realize that not to be so would allow the serpent of jealousy to invade our life. No one here is opposed to eros. It is a gift from God. But we can't take the chance of being unworthy of it."

"Hmm. I understand," Didi said, "more or less." She then tucked into the inviting meal.

In a minute they were joined by a very stout bald man named Brother Samuel. He was carrying an enormous pitcher of apple juice for the table.

"Brother Samuel," Brother Thomas explained, after the man had sat down next to Abigail, "is our horticultural expert."

Brother Samuel laughed. "Agrarian expert is a better term. We have few flowers here. Present company notwithstanding." And he made an attempt at a gallant bow toward the beauty of the two young women.

"In his previous life, Brother Samuel was an advertising copywriter. And a very good one at that," Brother Thomas noted.

Brother Samuel beamed and poured apple juice for all.

Then they were joined by a Brother Lawrence. He was a fierce-looking man about forty-five, with three fingers missing on his right hand. In a minute Sister Pia joined the group. She was quite young and wore her hair loose and long. And finally Sister Ruth arrived, whom Brother Thomas proudly introduced as "Keeper of the Beasts," a phrase Didi did not understand at all until she saw that the moment Sister Ruth sat down several German shepherds who had been eating along the perimeter raced over to pay their respects to her and then raced back to their food.

"Are you their trainer?" Didi asked the middle-aged woman with a leathery face and short-cropped gray hair.

"Either I am theirs or they are mine," she retorted happily.

Now the table was crowded, but Didi felt no sense of discomfort, no sense of being hemmed in. In fact, for some odd reason she felt that she had known these strangers a long time, as if it were some kind of homecoming for each and every one of them. There was little conversation while they ate. There was in fact a great stillness in the tent. Suddenly Didi had a wild thought—that maybe this was the way it was at the Last Supper. What a crazy thought! Since when did she think in religious categories? Oh, how strange it was. She stared at Brother Thomas hard . . . he was concentrating on his ratatouille. She never thought in religious categories even though her mother had been a devout Roman Catholic and her father had been one of those pious German Moravian Protestant souls who refused to curse, lie, cheat, steal, hate, or bear arms. Her father had died when she was young but her mother used to tell her stories about him; about how, even when the wolf was tearing at his throat he would not defend himself, nor would he hate the wolf. It was only when she was grown that Didi realized the wolf was just a metaphor—no actual wolf had ever torn her father's throat.

Then, as each one finished, each one left. And Didi and Abigail and Brother Thomas were once again alone at the table.

Didi turned slightly to watch the men and women leaving the mess tent and returning to the fields. There seemed to be about sixteen of them—roughly half women and half men. The great majority seemed to be middle aged or over, though there were several younger people; surely that Brother Neil was one, and Sister Pia another.

As she watched them she felt an odd longing; but she couldn't identify it. It wasn't the desire for physical farm labor. For someone like Didi, who had grown up on a farm, that was romantic nonsense. No, it was something in the way they were returning to their work . . . their kind of motion . . . almost a musical, synchronized way of walking. No, she couldn't put her finger on it. And all this was getting nowhere.

"It is time, Brother Thomas, that Abigail and I go back to work," she announced.

"You mean you are leaving now?"

"Yes."

"I thought perhaps you would honor us with your presence for a few days."

"No! I'm a veterinarian! I have a practice to attend to!" Didi had retorted to his suggestion so violently that all parties became embarrassed. "I'm sorry I shouted, Brother Thomas. But I really must be going."

Brother Thomas said: "You could stay here and just attend to emergencies as they come up. Dutchess County is not that far away."

"Look, even if it was possible . . . I mean, I imagine it *would be* possible to stay here for a few days. I could call home and get some other vet to cover me for a few days, I guess. I do it often enough for them. But we didn't come here prepared. We don't have any clothes or . . . or anything. Not even a toothbrush. You see? So, thank you very much for your offer. But we just couldn't. Maybe some other time." After she spoke she stared at Abigail to make sure her companion knew they were leaving shortly.

"I'm sorry you can't stay. I would like very much to talk with you further," Brother Thomas said. "You seem to have a genuine curiosity about our religious faith. You seem to want to know what we mean by the term Spirit."

Didi realized this old man was very acute, very sensitive to the unspoken currents in other people. It is a great gift. Didi herself had it with animals—but not with people, never with people.

"And I think there are other things on your

mind, things that are fretting you . . . things that you need to distance yourself from." Didi was absolutely shocked at this comment by Brother Thomas. He seemed to have stepped over the line. What was he now? Her shrink? She stared for a moment into his very blue eyes. He seemed unaware that he had stepped over the line. Well, he was very wrong. Yes, in some ways she was unhappy, but she was doing the work in the world she loved the most— healing the animals.

She stood up abruptly and Abigail followed suit.

"I shall walk you to your car," Brother Thomas announced.

They walked together back to the main house. The afternoon air was heavy with the smell of the fields. Didi's denim shirt was damp with sweat and tiny flies were circling her brow. She brushed them away; they came back again.

"We can go through the house," said Brother Thomas. "It is quicker as the crow flies."

They climbed the back porch, reentered through the monks' wing, and headed down the corridor.

"Thank you again for the kindness of delivering your friend's gift in person."

"Actually, Brother Thomas, Mary Hyndman was my mother's friend," Didi corrected him stiffly.

"We get a lot of small gifts like that. Bequests. Often in cash. But sometimes it is not money."

"You mean produce?"

"That, too. But other items also. Here, let me show you." He stopped in front of the last door in the monks' wing, set back a bit.

He opened the door and flicked on the light. They were looking into a huge walk-in closet. Perhaps it had served as the main larder when the house was owned by a millionaire.

"Come, look inside," he urged.

Didi stepped in, followed by Abigail.

"Everything at Alsatian House is communally owned," the old man confided. "Even clothes. People contribute all sorts of garments to us."

Didi stared at the crowded but neatly arranged shelves. There were shirts and pants and sweaters and nightgowns, shoes and socks and jackets and slickers, caps and scarves and walking shorts and petticoats. All the genres were separated into three categories—small, medium, large.

And everything was freshly laundered; in fact, the room-size closet was saturated with that delightfully nostalgic odor of mild-scented bleach.

"And here are the toilet articles, also donated, also communally owned and used," Brother Thomas said.

"Are you trying to tell me something, Brother Thomas?" Didi asked.

"I think I am . . . in my clumsy fashion. I am telling you that your clothes and all your other needs are well taken care of if you choose to stay for a few days."

Didi glared at him. Why was this old man being so persistent? Why did he want her

there? Was it for her professional expertise—
was there something wrong with the dogs? Or
was he just an amateur shrink who had decided that she needed a rest . . . a chance for
some kind of spiritual recharging, like a cord-
less appliance. Or was he simply proselyt-
izing?

"It would be so nice to stay here for a while,"
she heard Abigail whisper, from behind.

Astonished, Didi turned and stared at her.
Abigail looked away and one hand began to
tug at her long golden hair. It was so strange
for Abigail to speak like that . . . to make a
request of Didi.

Didi started to respond with reasons why
they couldn't stay and then, suddenly, inexpli-
cably, her resistance collapsed. She felt weary,
terribly weary.

She turned to Brother Thomas: "Fine. We'll
stay a bit. Is there a phone here? I have to call
Hillsbrook."

"I knew it, Charlie. I knew you were up to
no good. I saw your face after Missy called.
Oh yes, I saw your face, Charlie Gravis." Mrs.
Tunney spoke with venomous accusation. Missy
was one of her names for Didi. Sometimes she
called Didi Miss Quinn, because that was
what she had called her mother. But she never
used Didi or Deirdre or Miss Nightingale or
Dr. Nightingale. In fact, Didi's mother had not
collected the retainers she had passed on to
Didi until long after her husband's death . . .
so the name Nightingale was only a shadowy
presence.

Charlie looked up from his small workbench which was situated in one corner of the old barn. The hogs inhabited the far side and their grunting was audible. It was growing dark.

"Well," Charlie said, moving bottles carefully about the top of the bench, "if the lady of the house is going to be away for a few days, I figure it's time some of the mice make some cash."

"You know she don't want you selling those crazy home-brewed medicines of yours, Charlie. You know that!"

Charlie, who considered himself one of the world's foremost practitioners of veterinary herbalism, arched his eyebrows, regarding Mrs. Tunney as the backward creature she obviously was, if she could characterize his medicinal art as "crazy."

"Will you listen to what I have to say?" Charlie implored, trying to deflect or blunt Mrs. Tunney's very considerable anger. Mrs. Tunney angry was a dangerous woman.

"I am listening," she announced, managing to make even that sound threatening.

"Do you remember Jake Brown's boy? Harry?"

"Of course I know the Browns."

"Well, Harry's got himself a horse. Not any old horse but one of these big beautiful gray ones that are all the rage now. You know the kind I mean—from Germany—Hanovers, they call them, I think. Yeah, that's the breed. Well, I'm here to tell you this one is big, over seventeen hands high. And get this . . . Harry thinks he's going to make the Olympics with that horse. In those three-day events for horse and rider.

"Now this horse, Mrs. Tunney, costs Harry's daddy more than one hundred thousand dollars—"

Mrs. Tunney interrupted violently: "Are you going to get to the point, Charlie? Or are you trying to mystify me?"

"Mystify" was the word Mrs. Tunney often used if she thought someone was trying to con her or cheat her.

"Okay, okay," Gravis muttered, then continued his story. "Harry works the horse about fifty miles a day. Walk, trot, canter, gallop. Every day. So, about two weeks ago the big horse breaks down. Miss Quinn and I go out. She examines the horse. Then she starts telling Harry what's the matter. Believe me, Mrs. Tunney, you never heard such nonsense. All that damn book learning. She says, if I remember it right, that . . . wait a minute . . . yeah . . . she says that the aerobic energy production was exceeded, so Harry's horse had to get energy by anaerobic pathways. Wait, Mrs. Tunney, it gets better. And then she says that the horse started producing lactic acid, which was . . . now listen to this, Mrs. Tunney . . . which was accompanied by fatigue."

Charlie let out a low groan as if merely recalling the event was not to be believed. Mrs. Tunney kept glaring at him.

"Then she starts talking about something called the failure of calcium release from something called the sarcoplasmic speculum . . . no, wait . . . it was the sarcoplasmic retic-

ulum . . . and by this time poor Harry has almost collapsed with fear for his one hundred
thousand-dollar import. So finally she says to
Harry that his horse is physically exhausted.
Yep, that was the final diagnosis. As if we all
didn't know."

He waited for a softening in Mrs. Tunney's
glare but there was no such thing. She did
say: "It's all that book learning that feeds and
clothes you and puts a roof over your head,
Charlie Gravis."

Charlie waved her comment aside with a
hand and continued: "Then she tells Harry
how she is going to fix his horse up. With so-
dium chloride and potassium chloride to re-
store hydration and a whole bunch of other
stuff."

"Are you ever going to get to the point?" Mrs.
Tunney asked.

"I'm coming to it now. This morning Harry
called. His horse kind of collapsed again.
Since Miss Quinn is away, I figured I'll go over
and fix up his horse for him and get some
cash. Everybody's happy and Miss Quinn
won't ever know."

He held up one of the bottles.

"You know what's in here?" he asked her.

"I know that it's trouble."

"Trouble, hell. This is a dynamite mix. One
teaspoon of pure honey to every tablespoon of
rosemary infusion. And it will do the trick because the real trouble with Harry's horse is
his heart. Horses that get exhausted get that
way because their hearts get weak. This I
know for sure. None of this nonsense with

electrolyte balances. The damn heart needs a boost. And this mix will do it. Believe me, Mrs. Tunney."

Mrs. Tunney shook her head slowly. Then she said: "Charlie Gravis, you're going to land all of us in the poorhouse." Then she turned around and strode out. Charlie mumbled under his breath and returned to his preparations.

Chapter 6

Didi smiled when she flicked on the light in her small room in the visitors' wing. Someone had done a bit of thoughtful "shopping" at the communal clothes closet and selected the next day's outfit for her: a green polo shirt, wide-bottomed jeans, brilliantly laundered white socks, and old-fashioned satin panties. The jeans, she noted happily, were decidedly out of fashion. There was also a bathrobe folded gently on the bed. She stepped inside and surveyed her new temporary home. It was much less austere than the monks' quarters in the other wing.

For one, there was a small radio and a lamp and a clock. And there were two chairs, not one. In addition, over the sink was a mirror.

She walked to the sink and tried the hot water. Well, it was lukewarm. Someone had also put a fresh bar of soap, a towel, a new toothbrush still in its case, a small toothpaste, and a clean but bedraggled hairbrush on one edge of the sink.

She looked at the clock. Incredibly, it was barely seven-thirty in the evening. But she was very tired. It had been a very long day:

thc drive up . . . the tour . . . the decision to
stay . . . the wonderful introductory lunch and
the equally wonderful supper. Yes, she was
awfully tired.

But she was glad she had made the decision
to stay for a day or two or three. The little
room comforted her. She felt free of the obliga-
tion of running the large house in Hillsbrook
and worrying about whether her charges had
done the chores properly. She also felt a kind
of delicious guilt at knowing she would not be
awakened during the night by someone who
thought his beloved horse or cow was dying,
when it was actually nothing more than a mild
case of gastritis.

More to the point, this serene, ordered place
seemed to blunt and soften the memory of the
horror that had set her visit to the monastery
in motion: the discovery of poor Mary Hyndman's corpse.

The daylight was rapidly fading. Didi walked
over to the single large window in the room
and stared out.

A tiny burst of sound came from her mouth.
She could see the river! She could see the
Hudson! Not a great dramatic swatch of it, but
the lawn on the side of the wing broke away
to a gradual drop and she could see a sliver
of water. It was, for some reason that she
could not fathom, thrilling.

There was a knock at the door. She turned.
Sister Pia was standing near the half-open
door. Didi realized that the long-haired woman
was not as young as she had first appeared
. . . not by a long shot.

"I hope you liked my selection," Sister Pia said, motioning to the piled clothes.

"Ah, it was you," Didi exclaimed. "Thank you very much. Yes, they are fine."

"If there is anything else you need please tell me. Don't hesitate at all."

"Thank you. I won't."

"And breakfast is usually served at seven. But if you sleep later you can always get coffee and bread any time."

Sister Pia gave a little wave and started to leave.

"Oh, Sister, wait just a minute, please," Didi asked haltingly, a little embarrassed at what she was about to do.

The other woman turned back.

"Have you been at Alsatian House for a long time?"

"Five years next month," Sister Pia said.

"That is a fairly long time," Didi noted.

"And every day of it has been a joy," Sister Pia said with great feeling.

"What did you do before you came to Alsatian House?" Didi asked and a moment after she had asked the question she felt bad; as fascinated as she was by the people at the monastery, she felt as if she were overstepping the bounds of inquiry now.

But Sister Pia was neither fazed nor discomfited by the question. In fact she broke out in a devilish grin, and said playfully, "Why don't you guess?"

"I'm sure I couldn't," Didi said. "Teacher? Seamstress? Candle maker?"

"Not even close," Sister Pia said. "Believe it or not, I used to be a rock 'n' roll singer."

"Really?" For Didi it was the most remote occupation imaginable for someone sequestered in a monastery.

"Not a good one but a wild one," Sister Pia said, still laughing. Then she waved her good night and was gone.

Didi left her room to look in on Abigail, whose room was just the next one over. But Abigail's door was closed and when Didi knocked there was no answer. After knocking again, she walked inside and switched on the light. The room was empty, but Abigail, too, had been provided with neatly folded night things, a starched pinafore and work shirt for the morning, and a selection of toilet articles.

Didi walked out, closed the door behind her, and went back to her room.

Just as she was about to shut herself in for the night she heard a weird noise outside.

She stuck her head out and looked.

Coming down the hallway was one of the most adorable German shepherds she had ever seen. He was not yet totally out of his puppyhood, so his feet were still too large for his body and his ears were still too large for his head and he moved with a kind of gallumping gait—not a trot, not a walk nor a run.

He shuffled right past a startled Didi, flopped down on the oval rug in the center of her small room, and began to take care of an itch.

"Well, well, well. You're not too shy, are you?" she spoke to the overgrown baby. "Just who do you think you are barging into my room like this?"

The dog stared at her, cocked his head, and then went back to his itch.

"I do believe I met some of your brothers this morning. They came flying in through a window. I don't know that I'd share my room with any of them. But you, Bozo," she said, giving him a silly name that reflected his silly, still oversized feet, "you are welcome to stay as long as you want." Upon saying that, she approached the adorable beast and scratched him behind the ears. He groaned in luxury.

Didi began to undress.

When she had pulled her shirt off over her head, she could see that Bozo had climbed up on the small bed and stretched out over the entire bottom half of the mattress.

"Now wait a minute, fella," she said. "I've met forward guys before but you really take the cake."

She walked over and pushed uselessly at his haunches in an effort to shoo him off. A low growl issued from his throat.

Didi stepped back. "Are you threatening me, Bozo?" she asked in mock terror.

Bozo realized his gaffe and rolled over on his back, big paws up, whining.

Didi was disarmed. "Okay, Bozo. Don't cry. Stay as long as you want. But I'm warning you: the first time I hear you snoring, you're out!"

Didi slipped into the nightdress provided and then shut the light off. She climbed into bed and pulled the light quilt up around her neck. July nights in Dutchess County were cool. In Columbia County they might be chilly.

Seconds later she was fast asleep, the soles of her feet pushed firmly against young Bozo, who didn't seem to mind it at all.

"So you've decided to stay."

The voice seemed to come out of the darkness. Abigail shuddered and stepped back a bit, out of the moonlight and into the safety of the porch. But then she saw it was the monk called Brother Neil.

"Yes, for a day or two."

"Was it the veterinarian who decided for you?"

"Yes."

"Do you work for her?"

"In a fashion. I live in her house . . . in her mother's house."

"From what I saw, she treats you like the village idiot," Brother Neil said.

He had come closer to her, but now Abigail shrank back from his words. "No," she protested quietly, "she doesn't do that." Then she paused and thought and said: "Well, everybody treats me a bit different."

"Why?"

"Because I'm—because people say I'm strange. Mrs. Tunney says there's nothing wrong with me except—" She stopped midsentence.

"Except what?" Brother Neil urged.

Abigail stared at the night sky. It was brilliant. She sat down on the porch steps, drew her legs up, and clasped her knees.

Her long golden hair kept falling over her face and she kept pushing it away. She seemed to be thinking about whether to continue speaking or not . . . about whether to answer the question.

Brother Neil sat down beside her on the steps.

"Mrs. Tunney says that I worry so much about what to say that when I finally say something, no one understands what I'm saying because what I was speaking about is long past."

Brother Neil laughed.

"But Charlie Gravis says that I make people nervous," she added.

"You don't make me nervous."

"He says that sometimes a whole day goes by where I don't say a word. That is not natural, he says."

The two sat together for a long time in silence, watching the night.

Finally Brother Neil spoke again. "Once your eyes get really sensitive to the dark you can see bats."

"Where?"

"Directly ahead, out toward the river. There are small caves along the river cliffs and the bats go out at night . . . in and out."

Abigail strained to penetrate the night but she could see nothing moving beneath the stars. There were mystery sounds, however, a quiet hum. Brother Neil moved his leg; it touched hers. She flinched just a bit but didn't move away.

"What is your friend's name again? I forget."

"Her name is Deirdre Quinn Nightingale. But everyone calls her Didi."

"I have seen a lot of young women like your friend come up here to Alsatian House."

Abigail did not respond.

Brother Neil continued. "They come to see our dogs but they become infatuated with something else."

"With what?"

"With the place . . . with the fields . . . with the peace that is here. And with Brother Thomas."

He clasped his hands in front of him and squeezed them.

"But much of it is an illusion," he said loftily.

"An illusion?"

"Yes. There is no peace here. There is no peace anywhere. The Spirit, as Brother Thomas says, always struggles against evil. And evil, as we know, is everywhere."

"I see no evil here," Abigail said simply. "You are all so nice."

Brother Neil laughed. "Do you know what Brother Thomas means when he speaks of the 'Spirit'?"

"I think he means love."

"No. The Spirit is what enables love to emerge, to heal. It is an invisible force that inheres in every human and dog and rock and cloud. It—" He paused and leaned back. Abigail could feel his eyes on her.

"Well, do you want to hear a story?"

"About what?"

"About Brother Thomas."

"Yes. I would like to hear it."

"I do not even know if it is a true story. And I never heard it from the mouth of Brother Thomas. But everyone here knows the story. It is part of the myth of Alsatian House."

Suddenly they heard voices coming from inside the big house. Abigail sensed Brother Neil tensing. The voices became louder, although one couldn't hear what was being said. Then all was silent from within.

Brother Neil continued.

"When Brother Thomas was a young priest he served as an army chaplain in Korea during the war.

"One of the units Father Thomas was assigned to was a military police company whose main job was to guard an ammunition dump.

"The MP's were supported by K-9 dogs. These were highly trained German Shepherds who walked alongside the armed sentries.

"They were trained to detect . . . trained to corner . . . trained to attack. And whether you like it or not, they were trained to hate Koreans. All Koreans—North and South. Dogs cannot detect subtle geographic differences. The North and South Koreans were the same people. You do understand what I am saying, don't you, Abigail? In that context, the dogs were trained to hate all Koreans so that they could detect the single infiltrator.

"It was a very large ammunition dump these dogs were protecting, and a very valuable one. The dump itself had been situated next to one of those swift flowing, treacherous rivers that punctuate the Korean landscape. The exis-

tence of that river made the dump easier to
guard because it was thought no one could
swim across that river or even boat across it.

"But one night a commando team of three
North Koreans did indeed swim the river in an
attempt to blow up the same dump.

"The two dogs on duty picked up their scent
and alerted the handlers. There was a general
alarm. The dogs were let off the leashes.

"They found and cornered the first intruder.
He killed one of the dogs with his pistol. The
other dog attacked and disabled the man.

"The second intruder was shot to death by
the sentries.

"Then the remaining dog tracked and cornered intruder number three. But he escaped
from the dog and ran for the safety of the river.
He was hit by gunfire from the sentries just
as he entered the water and vanished beneath
the swift-flowing water.

"The hero German shepherd who had saved
the ammunition dump and the lives of all
within was given a great deal of praise and all
the steak he could eat.

"Then a wondrous thing happened."

Brother Neil stood up suddenly and his
hand just brushed across Abigail's head, af-
fectionately. He pulled his hand away and
stepped back from her, receding a bit into the
night. But she could see him clearly, standing
there. He seemed to have become overwhelmed by the story.

He continued, still standing a distance
from her.

"Some time during the night the dog heard

moans coming from the river. He climbed the restraining fence of his kennel and ran toward the sound. The North Korean was not dead. Gravely wounded, he was struggling to hold onto a rock outcropping in the center of the river.

"The dog leaped into the river, swam out to the wounded North Korean, and dragged him to the shore.

"Then the dog licked the blood away from the man's wounds and tried to help him up. But the North Korean could not stand.

"The dog lay down next to the wounded man and stayed with him all night.

"The next morning the sentries found the empty kennel. They conducted a search. They found the dog on the riverbank with the gravely ill man he had saved.

"As the sentries approached them, the dog stood up and growled at them. He would not let them approach the wounded man, fearful that they would harm him.

"He was now protecting one of the wounded lambs in his flock.

"All that German shepherd dog had been taught . . . all his expensive training . . . all of it . . . vanished the moment he heard the moans from the river!"

Brother Neil came close to her again, quickly, and reached out and grabbed both of her hands and pressed them tightly.

"Do you understand what I am saying? Do you understand this very simple story? There is a spirit of love buried deep in every creature, in every blade of grass, in every rock . . . and no matter how you twist it and profane it and bludgeon it . . . a single instant of compassion . . . a single instant . . ."

He stopped talking and released her hands and stepped back.

"Do you know why I am telling you this story?"

Abigail shook her head.

"Because you are so beautiful."

Didi woke suddenly at twelve minutes after six in the morning. So suddenly that she frightened the big puppy, who leaped off the bed and stood by the door. Light flooded the room—a beautiful morning light. She had been dreaming that she was listening to some eerily beautiful music. But now that she was awake, the music remained. Was this some sort of nightmare? Was she dreaming that she was dreaming? No. No, she was fully awake now. And there really was music playing somewhere.

Bozo barked nervously and began to chase his tail.

"Okay, okay. Calm down," Didi said. She got up and opened the door for him.

He made his exit and padded down the hall.

"I knew you were just a one-night-stand kind of guy," she called out after him.

She didn't go back into the room because now she heard the music clearly. Someone was singing the old hymn, "Amazing Grace," in a style she had never heard before—a kind of bluesy swinging rendition.

At six-twenty in the morning!

Then she remembered the room at the end
of the visitors' wing. The chapel, she had
called it. But, as Brother Thomas had so mod-
estly described it, it was just the room where
people sing and pray.

Didi wrapped her bathrobe about her tight
and headed down the hall to the room. Halfway there she hesitated, realizing that she was
barefoot. Go back? No. What does it matter?
This was, theoretically, a place where only su-
preme values were practiced. There is absolutely nothing wrong with barefootedness. It's
downright pious.

She walked on, stopped just before the open
door and peered in surreptitiously. There were
a few people seated, scattered about the room.

Brother Neil was at the piano.

And it was Abigail who was singing.

Her rendition of that song, which everyone
had heard seven zillion times, was mesmeriz-
ing. Didi knew that Abigail was musical. She
had been told that Abigail had a lovely singing
voice. But she never expected anything like
this.

The sound was so beautiful . . . so holding
. . . so pervasive . . . that Didi felt a chill. She
clutched the top of her robe against her
throat.

And Abigail! How strange and glorious she
looked. She was wearing some of the monastery clothes—a simple, long muslin dress,
washed-out red, and over it, a pink sweater
with sweet little rosettes at the neck. Her hair
was pulled back and fastened with a rubber

band. She stood absolutely still as she sang, her face tilted up, her hands folded.

The only time she moved her body was when she turned periodically to glance at her accompanist, the pianist, Brother Neil, who smiled in response.

It was obvious Abigail had made a friend. And it was obvious that the atmosphere of the monastery had catapulted Abigail out of her shell. That was very good. The trip was turning out splendid.

Didi walked quietly back to her room, not even minding the cold tiles under her feet. She was happy and at peace.

But then a sobering thought intruded on her serenity. It was enough to stop her in her tracks. Once before, she remembered, Abigail had been drawn out of her shell. That had been disastrous, because she had become involved with what turned out to be a very evil young man. What if Abigail got in over her head emotionally? What would Didi do? How would she handle it? After all, Abigail, like the other retainers back in Hillsbrook, was her responsibility. There was that word again. It was a strange business, this being responsible for other people. It wasn't something Didi felt too well suited for. Certainly, she didn't revel in it the way some authoritarian types seemed to.

She suddenly stopped the flow of all those weighty thoughts and shrugged her shoulders, then continued walking. That unhappy episode in Abigail's life was then. This was now. And besides, Brother Thomas had assured her that everyone within Alsatian House was celibate by choice.

Didi closed the door of her room and started to dress in her borrowed finery.

The moment Allie Voegler's unmarked police car went north of Shawmut Lane he was in the poverty-stricken area of Hillsbrook called the Ridge. And he put all the car windows up.

This was a standard precaution. In the Ridge, just about anything might come hurtling in through the window of a cop car. A rock. A bottle. A pellet from a BB gun. Rotten fruit. Just about anything. Because the people of the Ridge hated the Hillsbrook Police Department.

There was good reason for the enmity. Whenever a dog vanished in Hillsbrook, it was said that Ridge People had stolen it and sold it to a lab. When a horse or a cow died suddenly and mysteriously, Ridge People were always blamed. When a car was stolen from one of the grand houses or estates in Hillsbrook, the finger was always pointed to the people on the Ridge. Rumor was, they chopped the cars up in the hills and sold the parts downstate.

So the Hillsbrook Police were always making sweeps through the Ridge, looking for stolen property or animals. And when they couldn't find what they were looking for they handed out summonses for burning garbage without a village license or some similar offense. The people of the Ridge hated the Hillsbrook Police, and the police in turn often hated them.

Allie pulled up in front of the Ledeen trailer.

It was early in the morning, still, but there was a smudge of smoke in the air, as if many cooking fires had been burning. He stepped out of the car and locked all the doors; then he made sure the trunk was locked. It was best to be careful in these parts if you didn't want to lose your jack and spare tire.

He started toward the trailer but a voice stopped him. Ledeen had called out to him. But he was standing on the other side of the road where five or six rusted shells of cars and pickup trucks lay. He seemed to be digging for something with a pickax.

Allie circled the car and crossed the road. In his hand he held a paper bag.

"Good morning, Mr. Ledeen," Allie said politely.

Ledeen spat onto the road. "That's what I said to you when you pulled up," he noted.

"So I'm returning the pleasantry," Allie retorted.

"Ain't that sweet," Ledeen said sardonically, lapsing into one of his upstate drawls.

"I want you to take a look at something, Mr. Ledeen," Allie Voegler said, moving closer and reaching into the bag. Ledeen buried the pick into the ground, wiped his hands on filthy overalls, and folded his arms.

Allie pulled out one of the aluminum foil-wrapped pork chops. He carefully opened the foil and held it out. "Take a look at it, will you please."

"I am looking."

"What do you see?" Allie asked, knowing this was going to be like pulling teeth.

"Looks like a pork chop," Ledeen said.

"It sure does, and you'll also agree with me, Mr. Ledeen, that it isn't store bought."

"Too thick."

"Right. And untrimmed."

"You looking for someone to cook it for you?" Ledeen quipped.

"No, I'm looking to find out where it came from."

"Came from a pig," Ledeen said, still in his comedy routine.

"Right. I figure probably one of your pigs."

"Don't think so, Officer."

"You do raise hogs, don't you, Mr. Ledeen?"

"I don't raise hogs. I keep hogs," he replied angrily, although the distinction was lost on Allie.

"Did you give these pork chops to Mary Hyndman?"

"I don't sell pork chops. I slaughter a few hogs each year to feed my family. There ain't enough meat to go around, so why would I sell it outside . . . let alone give it to someone?" He picked the ax up again. "That would make me a fool, wouldn't it? To sell meat when my family don't have enough to eat."

Allie knew he was getting nowhere. He had to take the gloves off. "These your junk vehicles?" he asked him.

"Guess they are."

"They're on the wrong side of the road, aren't they? I mean, this isn't your property this side of the road. It's posted. Maybe you better get these wrecks on to your side of the road or I'm afraid I'm going to have to give you a couple of summonses."

Ledeen buried the pick into the ground with all the strength and anger in his body. He glared at Allie Voegler. "You're trying to tell me something, aren't you, Mr. Police Officer?"

"I guess I am, Mr. Ledeen," Allie said. He rubbed one foot against the other to make sure he hadn't forgotten to wear his ankle holster. No, it was there, and the weapon snug in it. Just in case.

"Maybe I better look at that pork chop again," Ledeen said.

Chapter 7

Didi chewed her muffin carefully, much more carefully than she usually did. But the muffin was so delicious . . . so absolutely fresh-baked delicious that she wanted to know what was in it. What was the fruit? It tasted at first like cranberry . . . then boysenberry . . . then something else. She just couldn't place it.

She was alone at the table. Abigail had stopped by, eaten quickly, and left without saying a word to Didi about her concert in the monastery. None of the brothers or sisters seemed to linger over breakfast. They ate and rushed out to the fields as if they were guilty for their night's sleep.

"May I join you?"

Didi looked up. It was Sister Ruth. She carried a coffee mug and she was wearing a leather rodeo-style vest heavily decorated with American Indian designs.

She sat down across from Didi. "I thought you would like to watch one of our training sessions with the dogs," she said.

"Oh, yes, very much so. When?" Didi replied.

"As soon as I finish my coffee," Sister Ruth said.

"How many dogs are there on this property?" Didi asked. "I keep seeing more and more."

"Probably about twenty. At this time. We usually deliver and nurture and place about three litters a year."

"Is there still a long waiting list for Alsatian House puppies?"

"Very long. People are always complaining. But what can we do? In fact, every year three or four people try to bribe us. As if the money means anything to us."

"But you are paid for the puppies you place, aren't you?" Didi asked, trying to clear up the confusion in her mind about the placement of the puppies. She remembered what Rose Vigdor had told her: the puppies are not *sold.*

"Sometimes. We once gave a puppy to someone who sent us a nine-dollar money order three years later. And once we received nine thousand dollars from a person who adopted one of our dogs. But our puppies are not for sale. We place them with people we think will love them, who need them. It is as simple as that. There is no elaborate selection procedure. No nothing. And above all, no fee. Whoever wants to give money to Alsatian House— or give anything else, for that matter—can do so."

"It's amazing, the demand for your dogs," Didi said.

"Why do you call it amazing?" Sister Ruth snapped. She was obviously very upset by the question, as if Didi did not believe Alsatian House dogs were special.

Didi didn't say anything. The fact was, she didn't think there was anything so very special about the dogs. They were beautiful-looking German shepherds, obviously healthy, self-sufficient. But a wait that stretches into years?

"It's the temperament of our dogs," Sister Ruth affirmed. "That's why people wait five years for one. There's no more gentle German shepherd on earth than those born at Alsatian House. And the reason is simple. We don't train them with reward and punishment . . . like heaven and hell. We train them through their imprinting instinct."

Didi held up her hands to stop the woman's fascinating explanation. "Wait. You've lost me. You lost me at the reward-and-punishment stage."

Sister Ruth drained the coffee cup in a dramatic gesture, with an expert flick of her wrist, as if it were a shot glass of whiskey. "Come along. See for yourself."

Didi followed Sister Ruth through the fields, always moving away from the large house and the river, until they came to a grassy knoll.

"Ah, Brother Lawrence is already here, with Brother James, and the dogs. You've met Brother Lawrence already, haven't you?"

Didi nodded. "He lost his fingers at sea," Sister Ruth explained. "He used to be one of those dissolute merchant seamen. A kind of Jack London character."

Standing next to Brothers James and Lawrence was a mature shepherd bitch, and running about them were two very young dogs, almost puppies.

Sister Ruth stopped about twenty feet from the group. "You just stay with me," she told Didi.

Then she called out in a loud voice: "Come!"

The two men and the bitch walked to her, the two puppies, of course, following, and yapping.

When they were all standing next to Ruth, to the right of her, she called out: "Sit!"

Didi stifled her laughter as the two monks sat down immediately on the ground. The bitch followed suit. The two puppies looked totally perplexed, and then, playing the game, flopped down also.

Then she called out: "Lay down!" The two monks and the bitch followed orders. The puppies didn't know what to do but one eventually rolled over.

Didi realized what was happening for the first time. This Ruth was a brilliant trainer. She was integrating new puppies into a mixed pack—humans and dogs. The puppies would learn all the basic commands through mimicry, by following the verbally elicited behavior of the bitch and the two monks. No wonder, Didi thought, these dogs are so gentle and self-possessed. The distinctions are being erased.

Then there was the command to "sit" again and then to "stay" and then to "heel."

Sister Ruth worked them for only twenty minutes. And then the session was over. She turned to Didi, flushed, a bit triumphant, and asked: "Well, you see now? No heaven or hell. What do you think?"

"I'm impressed," Didi said. Then she added: "In fact, I'm more than impressed. I'm astonished."

Sister Ruth nodded her head.

Brother Thomas stared out of his office window toward the Hudson. He was watching the young visitor, Deirdre Quinn Nightingale, walk along the bluff. Accompanying her was Sister Ruth. They were deep in conversation. Brother Thomas smiled.

It was obvious to him that Sister Ruth had shown the veterinarian her training techniques and now they were probably discussing them. Well, Sister Ruth was an aggressive woman. In some areas she believed she held the truth in her hands. And the truth, she also believed, should be proclaimed.

Brother Thomas sighed heavily and removed the manila folders from the seat of his chair. He was ashamed of himself for having badgered the young vet into staying. But he liked her very much. She was the kind of person he had wanted at Alsatian House when he founded it eighteen years ago. She seemed skeptical, kindly, tough, pragmatic. But fate had not granted that. Alsatian House had never attracted people like this Nightingale; it had attracted instead the spiritually broken, the emotionally confused—frustrated visionaries.

Not that he was complaining about his fellows! No. The brothers and sisters were all the greatest blessing of his life. It was only that he had always longed for another kind of resident. Even if only to leaven the questing nature of the initiates.

Maybe, he thought, sitting down wearily, it was still the Jesuit in him, thirty some odd years after leaving the order, that made him try to "get" a Deirdre Quinn Nightingale. She *was* sharp edged, like a Jesuit. And mercurial. That, too, like his theology teacher had been, in the seminary. Father Waldheim. Yes, that had been his name. From Cologne. A brilliant, moody, mercurial man. Brother Thomas buried his face in his hands. Was he becoming senile? There was absolutely no relation between this young vet and that hoary old name from the past. Not gender. Not background. Not anything.

A soft but persistent knock on one of the doors made him sit up straight.

"Yes?" he called.

There was no answer. Brother Thomas raised his voice. "Yes! Yes! Come in!"

A shaken Brother Anthony walked in. He was a young man who had entered Alsatian House only a year ago—a handsome and confused young man who had spent his years between ages seventeen and twenty chasing chemical substances.

"What is it?" Brother Thomas demanded. The young man was terminally shy and words could only be torn from him by force.

"You must come quickly, Brother Thomas," he said. Then he took a long breath and added: "Something strange has happened to Therese."

Brother Thomas didn't tarry for a second. Nor did he say a word. He followed Brother Anthony out of the office, down the hall, out of the house, onto the lawn, and into the small wellhouse that stood to the rear of the parking lot.

This stone shed with a wooded planked ceiling now functioned as a hospice for the old dogs. When one of the monastery's dogs was too old or too feeble to be in the general population, they were brought here to be able to die quietly, at their own pace, with all the non-intrusive care they needed or wanted.

The only one there now was Therese; a sixteen-year-old bitch who had been one of Brother Thomas's favorite friends. She had been in a bad way for the past few days, almost comatose. Everybody was waiting for her to die.

Brother Thomas strode through the swinging gate of the wellhouse, followed by Brother Anthony. The floor was of stone and always damp, so fresh straw had to be continually strewn about for the resident beasts.

"Oh!" was all Brother Thomas could say when he saw Therese, and then he crossed himself.

"What do you make of it?" Brother Anthony whispered in his ear.

Therese was standing up! No one ever thought she would be alive still, and now she was standing up. She still looked ill and emaciated but she was standing up and one of her eyes was clear and she seemed to be contemplating one of the two bowls that were always kept beside her . . . one with broth and the other with cut-up chicken.

"What do we do?" Brother Anthony kept on.

Brother Thomas finally replied: "We do nothing. We leave her be."

He turned around and marched out, Brother Anthony following. Those two young women who were staying at Alsatian House had obviously brought some kind of hidden gifts to poor Therese. That was what Brother Thomas felt. But he did not confide that belief in Brother Anthony. All he said to the younger man was: "Let us watch and wait and pray."

Rose Vigdor parked her battered 1973 Volvo at a broken meter on the main street of Hillsbrook.

She turned the engine off and said to the Corgi who was seated on the front seat staring intelligently out the window: "Okay, Huck, I'm depending on you to keep Aretha out of trouble."

At the sound of her name, Aretha, who was in the backseat, stuck her head into the front seat. Rose grabbed her nose. Aretha shook loose and retreated. "I don't know what I'm going to do with you, old girl," Rose said sadly, shaking her head.

Aretha was a very kindly animal, but for some reason, once in a parked car, she barked and lunged furiously at people who passed by—so threateningly in fact that she scared the bejesus out of children, bicyclists, and assorted citizenry.

There is nothing so fearsome as a German shepherd who appears for all the world to be in attack mode . . . who seems quite capable of hurtling through the glass window . . . who seems about to do just that. The frightened passerby would of course have no way of knowing that Aretha was really as tame as a teddy bear.

Rose consulted her shopping list. Only three stops were required, she realized: the superette, where she could stock up on dog food and possibly fruit, although she usually purchased her produce at roadside stands. She also needed pasta and canned tomatoes and hard cheese. The health food store, where she could pick up wheat germ as well as run riot among the various bags of chips. The post office, for stamps. It was not a heavy list.

She went to the health food store first, was greeted civilly, and proceeded to go on her chip-buying spree. She was gleeful at how health food companies were now spinning off the most bizarre kinds of chips . . . all progeny of the simple potato chip; may it rest in peace. There were tortilla chips . . . spinach and broccoli chips . . . there were sweet potato chips . . . there were buckwheat chips and rye chips and tree bark chips. There were hot chips and bland chips. There was even a sour cream and chive chip. Rose loved them all and gathered them into her basket.

Then she went into the ancient superette, one of the oldest stores on the street, and made the necessary purchases. The only deviation from the list was five large rolls of paper towels, which were on sale.

Rose liked shopping in the village. There was friendliness but no intimacy. The checkout clerk in the superette, a stooped, middle-age man with dusky hair, even asked her how her "project" was going. Rose imagined he meant the barn, and she replied: "Slow but steady." His response in turn had been wonderful: "That is the way things get done."

Then she went into the post office and she realized her luck had run out. There was a long line and it was moving slowly.

Her first instinct was not to wait, since the stamp purchase wasn't crucial. But, as always, she was so delighted and reassured by the small scale of the post office, incalculably different from the Manhattan atrocities called post offices, that she calmly took her place on line and waited happily.

There was only one clerk and one window. Unlike the urban post offices, there was no division of labor here. The single clerk took care of every kind of transaction. The line moved very slowly because every postal transaction was inevitably accompanied by a chat between customer and clerk.

Rose was standing behind two high school girls. They were close together, reading a newspaper that one of them held.

Her eyes caught a headline:

HYNDMAN MURDER BAFFLES VILLAGE COPS

Rose remembered the name. It was the poor woman Didi had spoken of—the murdered woman.

Beneath the headline was a photo of Mary Hyndman.

Rose found herself staring at the picture over the shoulders of the girls. For some reason, the photo was oddly familiar. But Rose couldn't place from where . . . or why . . . or how the feeling of familiarity had surfaced. She surely didn't know any woman in Hillsbrook named Mary Hyndman.

Then the young girls folded the paper away and began to talk about their high school in very uncomplimentary terms. Rose wondered if it was the high school that Didi had attended. It had to be, she realized. There was only one high school near Hillsbrook.

The line was moving faster now. Rose purchased twenty-four first-class stamps and ten prestamped postcards. She went out to the car, found the dogs napping contentedly, and drove back to her home.

A pickup truck was parked in front of the barn. Lounging against the front fender of the truck—which was very beaten up even as rural pickups go—was a scrawny young man.

Rose recognized him immediately, although she had never seen him up close before. He was wearing a cut-down white shirt, jeans, and very decrepit boots. Handsome in a dark sort of way. But he had the affected sneer of the country boy busting to get out of the country, and that telltale slouchy posture, or lack thereof. Rose had noticed that all young men she encountered in Hillsbrook seemed totally exhausted. But from what? It did not appear there was that much to do in a town like Hillsbrook.

The dogs rushed out of the car to investigate him. They liked what they smelled, apparently. Aretha and Huck all but fell at his feet.

"You Miss Vigdor?"

"Yes. I am Rose Vigdor."

"I'm Trent Tucker. Miss Quinn told me you want to see me."

"Yes, I want to see you. But first, tell me why they call you Trent Tucker."

He straightened, confused by the question. "That's my name."

"I know it's your name. I mean, why does everyone always say your whole name—Trent Tucker—rather than just Trent—or Tuck—or something. People in normal conversation don't use the other person's entire name."

"They use mine, ma'am."

"Okay. Okay. Here's what I need: someone to take a big load of garbage, almost four months' worth, to the dump. Except for the wood, the garbage is all bagged. Are you interested in doing the work?"

"Yeah."

"Let me show you what's involved. Then we can set a price. It's all around the side of the barn."

Rose started to move off, then stopped suddenly, remembering. "The last time I saw Didi, she was on her way to Columbia County. How were the monks? Do you know?"

"Miss Quinn never came back."

Rose's heart froze in her chest. Never came back? Had there been an auto accident? What?

"She and Abigail are staying there for a day or two," he added.

Rose breathed easier.

"Well, let's get on with it," she said. "Come this way."

She led him around the side of the barn. There were two enormous piles of garbage—one bagged, the other, cardboard cartons filled with old wood slats removed from the barn, odds and ends trimmed from new wood, and shavings.

She had already started to describe the contents of the bags when she realized that Trent Tucker hadn't followed her.

Walking quickly back around the corner of the barn she found him staring up in wonder at her hastily constructed and rather precarious scaffolding.

She didn't like the way he was looking at it. She knew the locals thought she was a madwoman. In the abstract, that didn't bother her. But this young man was something else. "Is anything bothering you, Mister Trent Tucker?" she asked in a voice that dripped with the threat—if you give the wrong answer I will club you.

"No, just looking, ma'am," he said, "just looking."

She turned and walked back around the barn, Trent Tucker following her closely. He listened carefully as she described the garbage, then he just walked among the bags.

"Well," he said, "I figure I can't do this in less than three loads."

"I think you can do it in two," she said.

"No, ma'am."

"Okay. How much?"

He cocked his head to one side as if he were faced with a mathematical problem of great complexity. Rose grinned. She found his pose absolutely charming. Even if most of it was straight out of a James Dean movie. Absurd, but charming.

Tucker bowed his head, scratched it, and regarded her through his shamefully long lashes.

She found him more than charming—almost sexy. He began to scrape the ground with his foot. She wondered what it would be like to have an affair with a bona fide bumpkin. He folded his arms and began to rock back a bit on his heels, closing his eyes, thinking, but also watching her movements. Rose wondered if she would have to ask Didi's permission before seducing him—if it ever came to that. She wondered if Didi would mind.

"I figure—uh, eighty dollars, Miss."

"Eighty dollars!"

"Yes, ma'am. Three loads. Here to the dump."

"No way."

"I think eighty's a pretty good price."

"Fifty."

"No. I can't do it for fifty."

"Everything is all bagged and packed."

"I can't do it for fifty dollars, Miss Vigdor."

"Add another ten."

"No. Okay. For seventy-five dollars. That's fair. Seventy-five dollars for three loads to the dump. You can't get a better deal than that, Miss Vigdor. Not in this county."

"Deal." She dug into her jeans and counted out seven ten dollar bills and five singles.

Then they loaded the pickup together and Trent Tucker drove off. The moment he was off the property Rose went back to her car and began bringing her shopping into the barn.

Afterward, she went to the rear of the barn and pumped some spring water up. She drank it greedily from one of those large scoops. The day was very hot. She poured some water over her head and just relaxed as it trickled down.

Suddenly, standing there in the heat with the cool water coming down, she remembered where she had seen that woman whose photo was in the paper . . . that murdered woman, Mary Hyndman.

It had been in February. She had been driven out of her barn by a brutal cold wave and checked into a motel for a few nights with her two dogs.

The second morning in the motel she had gone for a walk with the dogs in the snow. It had been one of those glorious winter mornings. A fresh snow, a freeze, and then a slight thaw. It was icicle heaven.

On the road, or rather just off the road, there was an old woman walking, with two rubber-tipped canes. The woman seemed to be struggling greatly but in good humor.

She had smiled at Rose and stared at the dogs. Rose smiled back and kept walking, but the woman stopped her by raising a cane tip.

"Can I help you?" Rose asked the old woman.

"You can answer a few questions."

"If I can."

"First . . . did you ever read Konrad Lorenz's book *Man Meets Dog or Dog Meets Man*?"

"Yes. I did. But a long time ago."

"Excellent. Now do you remember the reason why he said he would never have any dogs again after his last one died?"

"No."

"Ah. Let me remind you. Something about that when he is walking alone in the garden he hears the footsteps of his dead dogs coming up behind him . . . all the time."

"Now I remember."

"Good. Now there is one other question. Do dogs also hear the footsteps of dead masters coming up behind them?"

Rose didn't know what to say. This old woman was obviously a bit befogged in the head. Or maybe just joshing.

Rose said in a friendly manner: "I will think on it. I will try and come up with an answer."

"Don't try too hard," said the old woman. "After all, it *is* a riddle." And then she had trudged off.

Rose drank some more spring water. Yes, there was no doubt about it. The old woman she had met in the snow was the same woman who had been murdered. I'll tell Didi when I see her again, Rose thought. She treated herself to one more head bath and then got to work.

*   *   *

Didi was hungry and happy. It had been an exhilarating day. In the morning she had watched with fascination the dog training and in the afternoon she had helped transplant tomato seedlings.

The main dish at supper that night made her even happier—almost ecstatic. It was wide egg noodles, cottage cheese, and butter. This was a dish that Didi hadn't eaten since her mother died. It had been her mother's most made dish for her family.

Didi sat down at the table and stared at it reverentially before her fork took that first noodle, speckled white from the large-curd cottage cheese.

As she ate she listened to an argument between Sister Pia, the ex-rock 'n' roll singer, and Brother Lawrence, the ex-merchant seaman with the mutilated hand. Sister Pia maintained that music is the most defining element in any culture—whether it be the culture of a primitive tribe or a supposedly advanced civilization.

Brother Lawrence disputed that. He said that the food of any given culture is the most important defining element. What food the people eat. How it is obtained. How it is prepared.

Didi silently sided with Brother Lawrence, but it was probably because, she realized, she liked the way he delivered his argument—with great force, simply, as if he pulled every word out of his gut. As to the argument itself, as to the debate on the merit, she was neutral. She loved music. She loved food. Either way she won.

After Didi finished another satisfying meal she excused herself and headed back to her room. The night before, she had slept eleven hours before being wakened by Abigail's hymn. Maybe tonight she could sleep as long and as well. It was a great boon to her—eleven hours of sleep. In Hillsbrook, in her own house, she rarely got more than five fitful hours.

As she was undressing a wonderful idea popped in her head. What if she could conduct and publish an epidemiological study of the dogs bred in Alsatian House. The study would cover at least five generations and all aspects of their lives. It could be done, she realized, because the dogs that were placed were always followed up by the monks. And many dogs simply spent their entire lives at the monastery. It would, she realized, be a landmark work. She was quite happy with her life as a country vet—that was what she always wanted to do—but there was no doubt that research had always fascinated her as well. If she could combine the two it would be frosting on the cake. She could see herself being invited back to the University of Pennsylvania as a speaker. She began to spin all kinds of fantasies inside her tired head. They were pricked by an ugly sound at the door, as if someone were drunk and trying to break in.

She put on her bathrobe and opened the door a slit.

It was Bozo . . . the dog.

"Are you back again?"

He gave a little whoof, pushed his way past her, and headed directly for the comfort of her bed.

"What a romantic you are!"

Didi turned the light out at eight. She was tireder and happier and calmer than she had been in a long time. She fell asleep instantly.

But this time she didn't get a good night's sleep. She was awakened four hours later. And it wasn't "Amazing Grace" that disturbed her—it was the shriek of police and ambulance sirens. Was the place on fire?

Dazed and frightened, she rushed out of her room, down the long corridor and out the back of the house.

People were running from the house to the fields. The sirens were louder. People were shouting. Dogs were barking.

Didi ran also. Then she stopped at the edge of a circle of people. She fought her way through.

In the center of the circle stood Abigail. Her wrists were handcuffed behind her. A state trooper held one of her arms with his right hand. In his left hand he held an ugly black object in a cellophane evidence bag.

On the ground, being loaded on a stretcher, was Brother Neil. His eyes were too wide open. His chest looked like Swiss cheese. He was dead.

Chapter 8

The field emptied out before Didi's eyes. They took Abigail away. In handcuffs. They took what was left of Brother Neil away. They drove off . . . all of them . . . the state trooper cars, the ambulances, the emergency fire vehicles.

And then the dogs lost interest and vanished. And then the brothers and sisters went back to the house, whispering, holding onto each other.

And then Didi was absolutely alone in the night. She was stunned and shivering with fear.

What in God's name had happened? How had it happened? What was going on?

"Are you the veterinarian?" a voice asked. Didi wheeled, confused. No, she was not alone. Two men were crouching on the ground like football coaches outlining a play. One of them had spoken to her. A wind was blowing now, a strong summer wind, half warm, half cool. One of the men stood up. Didi saw he had a badge affixed to his jacket lapel.

"Are you the veterinarian?" he asked again.

"Yes. Who are you?"

"Van Pratt, State Police, Homicide." He

stood up and approached her stiffly, as if the crouching had hurt his legs. He was a handsome young man, with silvery hair. He was very broad across the chest and very narrow across the bottom. He was wearing what looked to be a graduation suit. Overdressed, understyled.

"You arrived with this Abigail?"

"Yes. She lives in my house. Where have you taken her?"

"She is being booked and charged."

"For what?"

"Murder."

"Are you serious? Abigail?"

"Three witnesses saw her with the weapon, standing over the body." He stared at Didi, then repeated: "Three witnesses heard shots. Ran to the field. Saw this Abigail standing over Brother Neil, holding a weapon. That's all I'm saying."

"That's all you're saying?" Didi asked, furious, mocking the homicide detective.

"But I'll listen to anything you have to say," he affirmed.

"The only thing I have to say is that I want to see Abigail."

"When was the last time you saw her today?"

"At dinner."

"That would be in that tent over there."

"Yes."

"Did you know there was something between this Abigail and Brother Neil?"

"What do you mean? What don't you say what you want to say?" Didi asked.

"You know what I mean."

"Yes, I know what you mean. I have no idea what the relationship was between Abigail and Brother Neil. They had just met."

The other state trooper, also in civilian clothes, got up, walked over to Van Pratt, and whispered something in his ear. Pratt nodded soberly.

"Can you give me your address and phone number?"

Didi complied. Then a car pulled up and several technicians piled out. They carried small satchels. They staked out the area where Brother Neil had been found. For the first time Didi saw the bloodstains. She felt sick to her stomach. She headed back to the house but stopped on the steps and sat down heavily.

What was she going to tell Mrs. Tunney? And Charlie? And Trent Tucker? What could she tell them?

"Are you okay?" It was Sister Ruth at the back door.

Didi waved to her, signifying that she was fine. She wondered if Sister Ruth had been one of the witnesses the state trooper talked about. Didi heard no shots. It was the sirens that had wakened her. She felt something wet on her arm. Oh, it was Bozo. He had found her and stuck his nose on her arm. She scratched him behind one ear. He groaned contentedly and flopped down, laying his entire head on her arm.

She was strangely lethargic. She knew what she had to do. First call Allie Voegler and seek his help. Second, get hold of a good lawyer in

Hillsbrook. And third, the most important, go see Abigail.

"Maybe we're both still asleep, Bozo. Maybe all of this didn't happen."

It was three-thirty in the morning when Didi pulled up to the state police barracks in her red jeep. She went in the front way, got authorization, walked out and around to the back of the building where the cell unit was. She entered a series of three doors and she was checked at each; the last with a metal detector.

Abigail was seated on a bench. She was wearing what looked to be gray pajamas with some kind of stencil written across the back.

The moment Didi saw her her eyes filled with tears. It was like seeing a beautiful doe caught in some kind of lewd and vicious trap.

Didi sat down quickly beside her and said: "Don't worry, Abigail. Don't worry."

And then she felt totally stupid and pathetic for affecting such a simpering manner, acting like some TV sitcom mother, with a distressed human. She never would be so mawkish and naive with her animal patients.

The sad truth was that there was plenty to worry about.

Abigail didn't greet her. She didn't say a word. She seemed to be staring at something no one else could see. Didi recognized that Abigail was in shock.

"Tell me what happened, Abigail," she urged, squeezing the younger woman's hand. Abigail squeezed back, then slid her hand away and ran it through her golden hair. She has never looked more beautiful, Didi realized, and that fact frightened her.

Abigail began to speak, but her voice was nearly inaudible. Didi edged closer to her on the bench. Like two birds on a branch, she thought.

"It was dark," Abigail said.

"Yes, it was a dark night," Didi agreed, as if it was a night long in the past. But it was this night . . . they were still in the terrible night.

"He told me to meet him," Abigail said. Her voice was abstract. She was now looking intently at one of the whitewashed walls as she spoke.

"You mean Brother Neil."

"Yes."

"Where, Abigail?"

"In the field. By the northeast corner of the bean field."

"Had you met him there before?"

"No. But he showed me the spot during the day, as we were walking past, in the morning, when you were watching the dogs being trained. I saw you watching. We both did. He asked me what was I to you and you to me."

Abigail sat ramrod straight. She started to crinkle her brow as if she were terribly perplexed.

"You must tell me what happened," Didi said, urging her to speak more.

The girl nodded. Her pallor was unbelievable, as if someone had drained all the blood from her. "I went to meet him. I heard sounds. Shots. I thought someone was dove hunting in the fields. I thought that. But he was lying on the ground. There was blood all over. It stuck to everything. I saw something on the ground. I thought it belonged to him. I picked it up and brought it to him. I don't know why. He was dead. Then I saw what was in my hand. It was a gun. I remember the barrel was warm. Then people rushed all around us. They started to yell."

"Did you shoot Brother Neil, Abigail?"

"No."

Didi stood up. She knew one thing; Abigail did not shoot anyone. She knew it before she had spoken to her and she knew it with more certitude now. But there was a lot to do.

"I will be back later," Didi promised. "And your lawyer will be here shortly. We are all going to help. We are all your friends, Abigail." Abigail did not respond. Didi walked out of the cell block area and into the parking lot.

Allie Voegler's car was parked beside her red jeep. She opened the passenger door and slid in next to him.

"Thank you for coming, Allie," she said, with feeling.

"There's an all-night diner about a mile down the road," he noted. But he didn't start the engine immediately. He asked: "How is she doing?"

"She's freaked out, of course."

"I found out something I think you should know, Didi."

"What's that?"

"The weapon Abigail was holding. . . . Well,

it was the same kind of weapon involved in a recent homicide."

"A recent homicide? What are you talking about?"

"Didi, it could very well be the gun used on Mary Hyndman."

Didi was startled. "Mary Hyndman? What does she have to do with what happened up here?"

"Look, I just thought you should know."

Didi's voice rose shrilly. "Are you trying to tell me there is some connection here? That you think Abigail had something to do with Mary Hyndman's death? Is that what you're telling me?"

Allie didn't respond. He drummed on the steering wheel with his fingers.

"There's more, isn't there?" she asked, hostile.

Allie continued the drumbeat.

"Well, don't clam up now, Allie. You just made some kind of point. But what the hell was the point? Don't you leave me dangling."

"There's something else you should know . . . but if you're going to blow up . . . it'll wait."

She took great pains to modulate her tone. "I'm not going to blow up, Allie. I'm calm. Honest. And I appreciate your coming here. Just go ahead and say what you have to say."

"Okay. You ought to know that Abigail was sort of moonlighting on you. She was working for Mary Hyndman until only about a month before her murder."

The information both crushed and baffled her. It was like a doctor learning that the patient he'd told to pay no mind to a silly little cough had just dropped dead. At that moment Didi felt dreadfully ignorant about the world.

Chapter 9

It was not really a diner. It was more of a blockhouse with tables, attached to the back of a gas station that sold snacks and newspapers and cigarettes and sundries. There was no waitress.

Allie paid the station attendant and then he and Didi carried their hot drinks and donuts to one of the fake redwood tables.

They sat down facing each other and sorted out the coffee and the donuts. Black for Didi. Cream for Allie. Old-fashioned for Didi. Jelly donut for Allie. Two napkins each.

They were alone. It was that vacuum of the early morning between the night and the day people—everyone had vanished. The roads were empty. Everything was still. The man who took payment for the gas was fast asleep again.

"The whole thing is kind of strange, Didi. I went to Mary Hyndman's house and was looking for something cold to drink. Because I had worked up a thirst looking for that damn puppy."

"Did you find the puppy?" Didi asked.

"No. Nothing. Anyway, in Mary's freezer were

a bunch of pork chops. But I could tell from the wrapping and the cut that they weren't store bought. And I found that strange."

Allie bit into his donut, chewed it, then wiped his chin with the napkin. "Not more than two days old," he noted, and then returned to his story. "I decided to follow up on it. I went to Ledeen on the Ridge because I know he's a pig farmer. A serious pig farmer but an illicit one. At first he was uncooperative. But then he looked at the pork chops. He said, Didi, that he raised Durocs for food and he knew Duroc chops and these weren't it. He said it looked like Spotted Poland China meat. Well, Didi, there aren't too many places anymore that raise them. Other than *your* place."

"It was Charlie Gravis who sold the meat to Mary?"

"Well, Charlie says he didn't sell it. He says he gave it to Mary because he heard she was hungry."

Didi grimaced. That will be the day when Charlie Gravis gives meat away.

"And then old lady Tunney chimed in and told Charlie to tell the truth . . . that he gave the meat to Mary Hyndman because Abigail and the old lady had had a fight and Charlie wanted to soothe troubled waters. Abigail? Why would they fight? I got very curious, and I pressed them. And Charlie finally told me the truth."

He took a long draught on the coffee and gave Didi one of those devious looks, as if he were evaluating her for some kind of mental breakdown.

"Charlie Gravis told me that Abigail worked for Mary for a few months. Until, in fact, about a month ago. When they had the fight."

"What did Abigail do for her?"

"Cleaning. Cooking. Taking care of the garden. It wasn't every day. And it wasn't a whole lot of hours. Mary paid Abigail by the hour."

"Why didn't they tell me?"

"Charlie said you wouldn't have approved of Abigail working for Mary Hyndman when there were so many chores going undone on your own place. But they wanted the cash she was bringing in."

Didi felt very weary. She wondered how many other things went on in her house that she didn't know about. As for the pigs, she had been trying to get rid of them since she moved back home. But to no avail.

"And that's all there is."

Didi's anger flared. "Come on, Allie. That's not all there is. You told it to me like there was some kind of conspiracy. Like Abigail being in jail now had something to do with Mary's death. That there is some kind of connection. I don't know what you were saying, but you were saying something."

"I don't think I was," Allie replied.

"Sure you were, Allie. Were you saying that you believe Abigail did shoot that brother? Were you saying that Abigail murdered Mary Hyndman?"

"As I said, I don't think I'm saying anything other than telling you what I learned. The Mary Hyndman case is mine. I don't see anything implicating Abigail. She did work for

Mary. And when I get a chance I'm going to question her about that. As for what happened here . . . this is Columbia County. It isn't my case, Didi."

"Okay, okay. I'll leave you alone."

Allie reached across the table and grabbed Didi's hand, half knocking her coffee over. "No, Didi, don't leave me alone. I want to help you and Abigail all I can."

"I could use some help, Allie. I have to get back to Alsatian House and get some sleep and get a few things together to bring to Abigail. Could you hang out at the state police barracks until the Hillsbrook lawyer comes to get her out?"

"Sure. But listen, Didi. She won't make bail. Abigail is going to be there for a while. They'll bring it to the grand jury very fast. She'll be indicted. And I heard they're going for murder one. Beside, they're going to send her for psychiatric evaluation. And probably put her on a suicide watch." He released her hands and flicked crumbs off the table. Didi watched his hands. They were powerful. Not like a dairy farmer's, like a laborer's.

"Do what you can," she said softly.

The sun was up and she padded down the visitors' wing toward her small room and sanctuary. But as she approached her room she began to hear very strange noises—a kind of rumbling on the opposite end of the wing. In the chapel room, where Abigail had sung so beautifully.

Was it prayer? No. Was it sacred music? No.

She passed her room and as she approached the chapel she tiptoed the last feet and peered in very carefully. The entire monastery seemed to be assembled! All the sisters and brothers she knew and others whom she hadn't met. The noise simply came from the milling about and whispering. There were not enough chairs to accommodate all of them.

Then she saw Brother Thomas behind the piano. He was rapping for order. Didi pulled her head back and pressed against the wall.

He began to speak. She could hear him clearly from outside. It was obvious he was speaking with passion.

"My friends. As you know, I rarely preach. Nor will I preach today. I just want to speak to you. I want to open my heart to all of you.

"A dreadful thing has happened. Brother Neil has been destroyed. He has been taken from us. He has been murdered.

"And, my friends, to a great extent I am to blame. Two days ago we were visited by two lovely women. They came to bring us a gift of money from a friend. I asked them to stay with us. And stay they did. And wondrous things began to happen. There was a lilt in the air. Old dogs became less feeble. Their grace shined upon us.

"But, my friends, I had forgotten one thing. They were from the outside and we were of the inside. They sought freedom; we sought constraint.

"I do not blame them. I blame myself. The circumstances are clear. Brother Neil was in that field at that time of night because he wished to taste the forbidden fruit. He wanted once again to experience the joy and the beauty of sexual love."

There was silence. Didi could hear some movement. Brother Thomas was drinking water. Didi felt odd—light-headed. It was so bizarre. Brother Thomas was talking about her and Abigail. He was accusing her. Of what? Of loosing the sexual serpent in the garden? Something like that.

Brother Thomas continued:

"Do you all remember what the Lord said to His prophet Isaiah? Let me remind you. The Lord said *I will give you hidden treasures and the concealed riches of secret places.* Yes, that is what He said.

"Alsatian House, my brothers and sisters, has always tried to be that secret place. And we have succeeded. We have gathered you all in and you live together in love and kindness and work. And because we are that secret place we are open to other creatures—the dogs and the birds and even the slugs that penetrate the stalks of our plants.

"Oh my friends. Let us have no more such tragedies. Know what can be done in secret places like Alsatian House. And know what cannot be done. We are very human here. Very fragile. We must abstain from some things so that we can participate even more profoundly in other things."

There was another pause and the brothers and sisters murmured their assent.

Didi had heard enough. She might be Jezebel but she was also exhausted. She headed toward her room and sleep. Oh damn! She remembered that she had to gather up Abigail's few possessions; she would need a change of clothing. Not the clothes that had been loaned to her by the Alsatian House commissary but the possessions Abigail had brought—the clothes she had arrived in, and her purse. Did she have a purse? Didi didn't remember. She couldn't recall ever seeing Abigail carrying anything.

Well, there was only one way to find out. Didi opened the door to Abigail's room and walked inside.

Pain and blackness came so quickly she wheeled around and banged against the open door. Then she felt herself falling. And she kept grabbing at long-haired, black-faced ewes. But she couldn't hold on.

Chapter 10

Didi opened her eyes and winced. The side of her face hurt terribly. She touched it with one hand and found a cold towel on it. Then she realized she was lying down, on one of the severe little monastery beds, and there were people staring down at her.

"She's conscious," someone said.

"Give her some air," another voice urged.

The faces hovering over her seemed constantly to go in and out of focus.

"How do you feel?" Sister Ruth asked, staring down at her.

"Okay," Didi said weakly.

"We heard the thud," portly Brother Samuel said. "You must have just collapsed and your face hit the floor hard."

"We should call a doctor," said Brother Lawrence.

"No need for a doctor," Sister Ruth objected. "She's just under strain. It's understandable given what happened with her friend, Abigail— and all those other things."

"Can you sit up?" It was Brother Thomas who asked that question.

Didi sat up. Someone propped a pillow against her back.

"Please let me rest," she said. The brothers and sisters milled about for a while in the small room, and then filed out one by one, shutting the door behind them.

Didi fell asleep where she was sitting, a deep, exhausted sleep.

She woke close to noon, stiff, and still with face pain. She saw Abigail's bag across the room, on a chair. Yes, she remembered. Abigail had always carried that bag—half purse, half general carryall. It was made out of gaily colored wool with a long red strap—Guatemalan. Didi walked slowly across to the bag, opened it, and took out a mirror.

Her face was badly bruised. She put the mirror back into the bag. She looked into the bag. Odd. How neat it was. Little piles of objects. She walked back to the small bed and picked up the pillow. A clean white pillowcase. Odd. It was turned inside out.

She felt strangely lucid. First off, she knew damn well that she hadn't just fallen down and hit her face on the floor. She had been assaulted the moment she stepped into the room. Someone had knocked her down and unconscious with a blow to the side of the face. In one brief blurred second, before the pain and the darkness, she had seen someone or intuited someone. That she was sure of.

And she was sure that the person who had been inside the room, the one who had struck her, was searching for something. Abigail's bag had probably been riffled. Otherwise, how could anyone explain the neatness of the objects, piled up like on a grocery shelf. And the pillowcase. Someone had stripped the pillow to see if anything was concealed there and, in a hurry, put the case on inside out.

She felt herself begin to tremble, like the way she was when she first started practicing; when she came across a sick lamb or a sick calf that she couldn't treat because she couldn't make a firm diagnosis.

She leaned back. And what about those words of Sister Ruth when Didi had regained consciousness?

Sister Ruth had said that Didi was distraught over what had happened to Abigail. That was true enough. But then she had added "and other things," or words to that effect. What other things? How could Ruth know anything about her life? The only bad thing that had happened before Brother Neil's murder and Abigail's arrest had been the murder of Mary Hyndman. That had been very distressing. But how would Sister Ruth know about it, if that was what she was talking about?

Didi grimaced. Her face was hurting bad again. She started to breathe in and out, slowly and evenly, to regain control. She was scattering her thoughts all around and she had to focus.

Remember, she thought, what her professor Hiram Bechtold used to say in vet school. "The first responsibility of the vet is to look and look hard. What do you see? Forget everything else. What are you looking at? What is the horse doing? How is he standing? Look large first and then zoom in, like a lens. Eyes! Look! See!"

But there was no horse in front of her to study. All she had were a few half facts. Abigail went to meet a lover—or a would-be lover. The lover was murdered. Abigail was caught holding the weapon. Abigail's room had probably been searched.

Who would be interested in searching Abigail's room? It had to be the real killer.

Why? What was being looked for? She stood up and began to walk slowly about the room. It had to be something that would implicate the killer if found.

She paused. She felt a sudden surge of insight. Brother Neil and Abigail had known each other only a short time, but maybe Brother Neil had given her something. A note? A love letter? A piece of jewelry? Could the murderer have been a jealous lover? Why not?

Was Brother Neil a rake? Had he routinely met other women in that field? Had he thrown over his current flame to meet the beautiful new visitor, Abigail? Had he then paid the price for his infidelity?

The pain subsided. She sat down again and slowly began to work her jaw. If Brother Neil had been carrying on with another woman, it was her guess that it was Sister Pia, who was still a very handsome woman and not that old. Besides, hadn't she been a singer in a rock band? And weren't rock bands wild? Drugs and sex and god knows what. Didi was chagrined at her own conventionalism. It was the most ridiculous of clichés, she realized. For all she knew, most rock 'n' roll musicians were family values boosters, chaste teetotalers who had to cultivate their images as dangerous degenerates in order to keep the magazines and the gossip columns interested.

And what if Brother Neil was gay or bisexual? His lover could have been a male. Maybe that handsome young man who seemed to be Brother Thomas's secretary.

There wasn't much time, she realized. The wheels of criminal justice grind slowly, except when a young woman is found next to a dead lover, holding the smoking gun that killed him.

It was a few minutes before noon. Harold Tepper sat in his usual booth in the Hillsbrook Diner, having his usual early lunch: a grilled cheese sandwich and a cup of tea.

The diner was in an uproar. A radio station had just reported the murder of a monk at Alsatian House; and the suspect in the murder, who had been arrested, was a young woman from Hillsbrook. No names were released.

The druggist didn't say a word. He kept picking at his sandwich. He knew that Dr. Nightingale was going to Alsatian House to deliver poor Mary Hyndman's sock. But he didn't know when. It could have been her. It could have been someone else.

Jess, the waitress, refilled his teacup with hot water. "Isn't that the wildest?" she asked.

And she was off without waiting for an answer, although Tepper didn't have one anyway.

He looked out the diner window. The sun was popping in and out behind some clouds. He had the feeling that it would be a very long summer.

Tears welled up suddenly in his eyes. He directed his attention back to the sandwich. These damn tears kept arriving at the damnest times. He knew what they were—depression. And he knew he ought to go on a Prozac regimen. But he didn't.

In a weird way, he was kind of glad that Mary Hyndman was dead, even though it was a terrible sentiment to feel. But just seeing that old lady had torn the heart out of him. She was dying hard and she didn't want any help. Oh, she took the medicines from him, but it was always a struggle and she used all kinds of defenses.

The hubbub in the diner died down. Harold Tepper looked around. He knew all the people in there. He knew their families. And he had grown to dislike them all. They had abandoned Mary Hyndman just like they abandoned all the aged, the crazed, the sick. Tepper had always known that the much heralded small town ethos was a leaky sieve. But the last years of Mary Hyndman had brought it into sharp focus for him.

Mary Hyndman had once been a much-loved person in Hillsbrook. A whole generation of women sought her advice on a host of topics. She was like the village guru. You could depend on her for some kind of truth . . . not like the kind of pap one got in the churches and the newspapers and the schools. Mary had been in foreign climes, she had been in dangerous situations. She knew things. She was wise.

Harold Tepper pushed what was left of the sandwich away. He wanted to leave the diner but he didn't want to go back to the store. He leaned back heavily in his seat; that was another bad problem in being depressed—indecision. Sometimes he just couldn't make up his mind. He couldn't make even the most trivial of decisions. Do I put my right sock on first or my left one?

The waitress cleaned off his table and left a check. He wondered if Mary ever ate in the Hillsbrook Diner. He didn't remember seeing her there, not even when she was much younger.

He shook his head sadly. Yes, he missed her, thinking about her so much—but she had been a very difficult woman in her final years. Just take the medicines! If she would have applied for Medicaid she would have had all that taken care of. But she was too stubborn to apply.

"We have some fine peach cobbler, Mr. Tepper."

He was disoriented. He didn't know where those words came from. From Mary Hyndman? No, she was dead. Then he turned a bit in the booth and saw the waitress, holding a tray of food for some other booth. He waved that he didn't want any. Then he stood up and began the tedious job of laying out the tip.

*   *   *

Didi kept to herself but her eyes were wide open. She had to get Sister Pia alone. She watched and waited and followed the sister during a long afternoon. The brothers and sisters were polite but they obviously no longer wanted any part of her; Brother Thomas's sermon had taken hold. Young Doctor Nightingale was the serpent in their garden. They had been extremely kindly during that episode in Abigail's room, but now that Didi seemed fully recovered, the serpent was once again dangerous.

It was late in the afternoon when she saw Sister Pia leave the fields and head toward the house. Didi followed, waited five minutes after Sister Pia had entered, then went in and located the sister's room. She knocked on the door. Then she walked in.

Sister Pia was seated on a chair brushing her long hair. She looked quite alluring, quite worldly, like the older models in the ads in plush ladies' magazines.

"How are you feeling?" Pia asked in a friendly manner, gesturing with a hand that Didi should sit on the bed.

"Fine. Much better."

"The bruise will go away shortly," she said comfortingly, staring critically at Didi's wounded cheekbone.

"I was afraid you would no longer be friendly to me," Didi said.

Sister Pia brushed harder and laughed. "Well, Brother Thomas does go overboard a bit in his sermons. I really don't think you're the threat he makes you out to be."

"Thank you."

"How is your friend Abigail?"

"Greatly distressed."

"Yes, I would imagine."

"It is so absurd for them to think that she would murder Brother Neil. Abigail can hardly bear to walk lest she steps on an ant."

"Well," replied Sister Pia, "she was found with the gun in her hand."

"Yes, she was," Didi agreed.

Sister Pia changed hands and began to brush the other side of her head.

Didi tried to imagine the woman seated on the chair in her previous life—a hard-rocking, gravel-voiced thing in black leather and far too much makeup. A girl who took drugs at will, perhaps, and lovers.

"I thought," Didi said quietly, "that you might be able to help Abigail."

"Me? How?"

"Tell me something about Brother Neil."

"What is there to tell?"

"I mean something about his past. And something about how he was in the monastery."

"I don't really know much about Brother Neil's past. He was from the Midwest originally, I believe."

"Then what did he talk about?" Didi blurted out, suddenly unhappy with the course of the conversation . . . which was going nowhere.

Pia smiled sweetly—or was it sardonically? Didi couldn't tell.

Sister Pia placed the brush on her lap. "Let me see. What did Brother Neil talk about? You know, the usual things. Death. Eros. War. Peace. God. The Devil. Food. Manure." She burst out laughing. "Yes, he talked about manure a lot because that was one of his main jobs, making sure there was enough fertilizer for the fields."

"Were you close to him?" Didi asked.

"We're a very close-knit group here."

"Yes," Didi said, "I realize that. But I meant . . . I meant especially close."

"I'm not sure I know what you mean by that."

Didi paused. She didn't know if she should come right out with it. She didn't know what phrase to use.

"I meant—" Didi halted midsentence. Then she decided there was no time left for subtlety. "Were you and Brother Neil lovers?"

"Of course we were." Sister Pia's mysterious little smile had vanished. "We used to do it in the orchard—in the trees."

"I'm very sorry if I'm offending you," Didi said. "But I'm trying—"

"Yes, indeed you are," Pia spat out. Then she stood up and walked to the door. She opened it. "Good afternoon, Dr. Nightingale," she said. "Feel better soon and have a safe trip home—or wherever it is you go when you leave here."

"I didn't mean to upset you," Didi said.

"Please leave!"

"I just want you to tell me the truth."

"And I just want you to get out. Get out!"

She was starting to yell but Didi had to press her.

"Who wanted Brother Neil dead?" she asked.

And then Sister Pia began to scream. Didi ran out of the room. Sister Pia followed her, still screaming.

Brother Thomas appeared. He stared at both women. There was an awkward silence. Sister Pia was breathing heavily.

He looked from one woman to another for an explanation. Neither of them spoke.

"I think," he said to Didi, "it is time that you returned to your practice in Hillsbrook."

"Yes," Didi replied bitterly. "The serpent should be removed from the garden." Then she was sorry she had said it. This old man had been wonderful. "I will leave in the morning," she said quietly.

She started to walk away but Brother Thomas's hand stayed her.

Brother Anthony, the handsome young man who functioned as the old man's secretary, was coming toward them.

He was walking very slowly and holding out one hand.

"What is it? What is the matter?" Brother Thomas asked.

There was a wound on Brother Anthony's thumb. A jagged tear. It was bleeding profusely. Sister Pia stepped forward with some tissues and pressed down on it. The young man ignored her. His face was white as a sheet.

"Agatha bit me!" he said. "She's eating her children!"

Brother Thomas let out a groan and started to walk quickly down the hall. The others followed him. Soon the old man was running as best he could.

Chapter 11

Just as Brother Thomas opened the door, Didi heard the snarl and cried out—"Get back!"

But it was too late. Eighty pounds of enraged German shepherd motherhood hit him square in the chest and sent him reeling backward, almost sending both Brother Anthony and Sister Pia to the floor.

The face of Agatha sent a chill through Didi. It was the full attack mode—a mouth open, ears forward, fangs bared, lips curled snarl.

But Agatha did not press the attack. Once she had routed the intruder she trotted back into the room.

Didi surveyed the scene with a practiced eye. The monks had obviously turned one of their cells into a whelping room for Agatha. Everything had been removed and the floor covered with straw mats and newspapers.

It was a sad and ugly scene.

Agatha had dropped four puppies. All of them had obviously been born dead.

And one of them had been born deformed. That was what Brother Anthony had been talking about. For the deformed puppy had been half eaten by Agatha. But this was perfectly natural.

Didi could see that Agatha was in a very bad state. She did not know the puppies were dead.

She kept licking them as all bitches do.

Didi called out to her softly: "Agatha, girl."

The bitch wheeled and snarled. Then she began to run back and forth across the room, leaping against the walls.

Then she picked up the puppies one by one, gently, and brought them to one corner of the room. Then she picked them up one by one and took them to the other side of the room.

Then she started to climb the walls again. She began to cry, snarl, chase her tail, pick up the dead puppies again.

"We have to get her calm," Didi whispered to Brother Thomas. "Do you have any Valium?" Brother Thomas shook his head. Didi silently inquired of the other two. They both shook their heads. Didi cursed herself for not bringing a basic bag of veterinary supplies. But she hadn't known she would be staying. The idea was just to deliver Mary Hyndman's money.

Sister Pia blurted out, "There may be some in the infirmary. And there may be some in Brother Neil's room."

Didi took charge. "You go to the infirmary," she said to Sister Pia, "and I'll look in Brother Neil's room."

To Brother Anthony she said: "I'm going to need a big bowl of heavy cream. Do you understand? And some sugar. Can you get that for me?" He nodded and left.

She turned to Brother Thomas. "Now I'd like you to stay right here. But don't enter the room like you did before. Understand? Just remain here. Try not to move about. Leave the door just as it is." Brother Thomas replied: "I'll do exactly as you say." She could see that the sight of the dead puppies had profoundly affected him. "You do understand, Brother Thomas," she said, "that Agatha didn't kill her puppies. They were born dead." He didn't reply. She continued. "And I also hope you understand that it is common procedure for a bitch to kill and eat deformed puppies." Again, he didn't reply. Didi didn't have any more time for him. She walked, almost ran down the hallway.

Once inside Brother Neil's room she reflected on the irony of monasteries—their rooms are so spartan one cannot tell whether the occupant is alive or dead. If there was Valium in this room, and Sister Pia must have known something if she suggested it—it could only be on, in, or under three objects. Because that was all there was in the room. A chair. A bed. A small chest.

First she went to the bed, picking up the mattress and shaking out the pillow. Then underneath the seat of the chair. There was nothing there but splinters. She inspected the top of the seat—it was seamless.

The chest. It had five drawers. The first drawer contained Brother Neil's paper remains—a calendar, a few letters, a pen and four pencils, three of them unsharpened. A twang of familiarity came to Didi and she was perplexed, staring at the objects until she realized the neatness of their placement reminded her of the objects in Abigail's bag after the bag had been ransacked. Didi's hand went to her face. In the excitement over Agatha she had totally forgotten her bruise, and in fact there was no pain. She touched the side of her face gingerly. The pain, she knew, would come again and the bruise was just beginning to rise. She would look much worse before she would look better.

The second drawer had absolutely nothing.

The third drawer had a pair of leather slippers.

The fourth drawer had a small white envelope. Didi smiled. She opened the unsealed flap and shook out the contents.

Yes, they were pills. But they weren't Valium.

She picked up the pill. It definitely was not Valium or anything in the benzodiazepine family.

She turned the little green pill over in her hand. A pretty little pill. She smiled at the memory. It was dexamyl. The Rolls-Royce of student helpmates.

Good old dexamyl. Speed cut with aspirin. She had used it that first terrible year of vet school when she needed to write and study and she just couldn't get with it . . . she couldn't focus . . . she couldn't stay awake . . . she couldn't get out of that depression.

Didi let the pill fall back into the drawer. How odd it was for Brother Neil to have used dexamyl! Why? It wasn't the kind of substance that one would think would be found in a monastery.

She hurried back to Agatha's whelping room. Sister Pia called out in an exaggerated whisper as she approached: "I have three. Three." She was holding the pills in her clenched fist.

"Fine. That'll do it," Didi said.

Then Brother Anthony arrived carrying an enormous basin and an enormous pitcher—old-fashioned enamel objects. His face was utterly void of animation. His movements were quick, efficient, but he might have been a robot.

"Put the basin on the floor and pour cream into it," Didi said, helping him. "And then put the sugar in—about a cupful—and mix it."

Didi turned to Brother Thomas. "I'm going to go into the room and pacify Agatha. The moment you see that she is quiet I want you to quickly remove all the puppies from the room. Do you understand?" Brother Thomas nodded.

Didi took the three Valium pills from Sister Pia. Then she picked up the basin of sugar and heavy cream and entered the room.

Immediately she was faced with a snarling, lunging, hysterical bitch. But Didi held her ground and inched forward until she was deep into the room.

Then she began to speak to Agatha in a low voice. "Now, now, Agatha . . . why do you want to bite me . . . you know I'm your friend . . . don't you . . . if you bite me there's going to be blood and I hate the sight of my own blood.

Besides . . . look at the side of my face, Agatha
. . . haven't I got beat up enough?"

Didi knelt down and placed the basin of
cream on the floor.

She dipped both of her hands into the thick
white liquid and pulled them out dripping.

She held the dripping hands out to Agatha.

The bitch attacked again in a fury but at
the last moment the smell of the heavy cream
slowed her down. She stopped, confused. She
sniffed. She snarled. She tentatively licked one
of Didi's hands. And then she began to lick
the cream off.

All the time Didi kept talking to her and re-
dipping first one hand and then the other into
the cream. The bitch seemed insatiable.

Then Didi deftly slipped a Valium onto the
bitch's tongue as she licked. Then another.
And finally the third.

Brother Thomas came into the room. Then
the others moved in. They inched forward,
pressing their backs against the wall. Didi saw
them pick up one dead puppy, and then another, and another. And the mutilated one.
Slowly, they inched out.

Agatha was slowing down. She was now sitting and licking. Soon she lay down. Didi kept
feeding her the sugared cream. She stretched
her muzzle across Didi's lap. Didi stopped
talking to her and just stroked her behind the
head. An exhausted Agatha, warmed by the
cream, calmed by the Valium, fell fast asleep.

Didi extricated herself and walked out of the
room. Brother Anthony had left to dispose of
the puppies. "Just leave her alone," Didi said

to Brother Thomas and Sister Pia. Brother Thomas nodded. Brother Lawrence and Sister Ruth were coming down the hall. Didi stared hard at the old man for a second. She wondered whether he thought Agatha's misfortune was also because of her . . . the serpent. Her face began to hurt again. And she was so tired. More tired than Agatha.

She walked slowly back to her room in the visitors' wing. Bozo followed her in and climbed up immediately on the bed. She sat down beside the somewhat goofy puppy who was momentarily entranced by the new smells on her and the flecks of sugared heavy cream.

"Well, Bozo," she said, "our affair is over. I'm leaving in the morning." Bozo didn't seem concerned at all. Didi pulled at one of his ears. "There's always another bed for you. Is that it, Bozo?"

Bozo decided that she wanted to play. He rolled over and lifted his two front oversized paws. "I can't play with you, Bozo. I'm too tired. In fact I can't play with you until I find out who murdered Brother Neil. But, Bozo, how can I find that out if Brother Thomas wants me out of here? Tell me, friend, do you think I'm the serpent in paradise?"

He gave one of his puppy grunts and whacked her on the shoulder. I suppose I deserve that, Didi thought, for talking disjointed nonsense to a dog. Then she stretched out and, fully clothed, fell fast asleep.

She woke from a deep sleep with a start. She had forgotten she was wearing her clothes. It was pitch dark in the room. The luminous clock in the room read four o'clock. Didi couldn't believe it. Had she slept twelve hours straight? Yes, it was obvious she had.

And Bozo was still fast asleep, having some kind of spectacular canine dream—twitching and moaning, with his REMs going ballistic.

She closed her eyes. It was too early to leave. She had planned to check into a motel and then go to visit Abigail. She really didn't know where to go. Not back to Hillsbrook, leaving Abigail in the lurch—though sooner or later she would have to go back—she had a practice.

She kept opening her eyes, staring at the clock, then closing them again. Obviously she was slept out.

As for getting up and packing—there was nothing to pack, just Abigail's carryall.

Lying there and thinking back over the past, quite incredible twenty-four hours, she had trouble recalling what happened when. Everything seemed mixed up time-wise. The murder of Brother Neil happened after she was struck in Abigail's room. And Agatha's misfortune happened before Brother Thomas's speech on the serpent in their midst.

My circuits are overloaded with mayhem, she thought, like a deer who is worried by a pack of feral dogs and who ceases to run from them—just falling down because the stress is too much.

She remembered, lying there, with chagrin, her interview with Sister Pia, the one that had ended in screaming and in Brother Thomas asking her to leave.

How unprofessional of her. It was a most pathetic attempt at a criminal investigation—like using a fire hose as worming medicine.

She almost fell asleep again, but Bozo's thrashing about aborted it. Then the big puppy awoke and wanted to go out. She let him out. Five minutes later he was scraping at the door and she let him in again.

At five-thirty there were the first inklings of dawn and she decided she might as well leave. What was the point of prolonging it?

"Travel light, Bozo," she said, picking up Abigail's bag and heading toward her own tote-bag, which was at the foot of the mattress.

Bozo knew something was up and he stood straight up.

"Yes, Bozo, the affair is over. I am afraid I am going to be leaving now. But remember, Bozo, it was nothing you did."

She leaned over and caressed the big puppy. He licked her face. It was like being doused by a sponge.

Suddenly Didi remembered that she had slept in and was still wearing monastery clothes. She went into her carryall, brought out the clothes she had come with, undressed, put her own clothes on, and left the monastery clothes folded carefully on the chair.

"Will you write, Bozo?"

Bozo cocked his head and sat on his haunches.

"You devil. You say you will but I know you won't. I know that the minute I leave you'll shrug your ears and find another bed. But I still love you, big guy."

Then she leaned over to close the carryall.

But Bozo prevented her, placing both front paws firmly into the open bag.

"I can't play now, Bozo. I have to go."

She gently pushed him away. He growled menacingly.

"What is the matter with you!" she demanded, standing up and stepping back angrily.

Bozo stuck his face into the bag, rummaging about with his nose. He pulled something out in his jaws and started to prance about the room with it. Then he sat down in one corner, happily guarding his treasure.

Didi stared at the object, wide-eyed. It was Mary Hyndman's sock. The old black wool sock that had contained the money.

Didi's stomach flipped over. She understood what she was seeing. Bozo had been Mary Hyndman's puppy!

Wait! Didi cautioned herself. Wait a minute! Her veterinary training demanded that she not jump to such a wild conclusion over one lousy sock.

She walked to the door, turned, and looked at Bozo. He kept at the sock.

She had to think this out. She had to be sure. Because that brief moment of revelation, she knew, could open up a very large can of worms. If the revelation was really that.

She watched Bozo carefully as he worried the sock.

She remembered a fascinating article she had read only about two months ago. It had been written by a veterinarian and a science reporter. The piece explored whether there was such a thing as heritable behavioral characteristics in dogs.

The article had paid great attention to German shepherds because of what was happening in the world of guide-dogs for the blind. Up to the 1970s, the breed most used for that kind of work was the German shepherd. But slowly they were weeded out. Now, today, the dogs of choice are labrador retrievers and golden retrievers.

Why did this happen? the authors asked. The answer was simply that more and more shepherds were showing traits of nervousness—unacceptable levels of nervousness. Had this nervousness become a heritable trait because American breeders were trying to produce show dogs rather than working dogs? Or was it because puppies were being placed too late in homes? Or too early?

The article then went on to contrast the growing disuse of German shepherds in guide-dog work with the continuing success of the breed in tracking.

The writers had quoted all kinds of recent studies showing the remarkable ability of shepherds in tracking tests, particularly tests with the dogs' ability to discriminate between identical human twins and their objects.

Didi didn't remember the article's conclusions about whether the ability to scent well was heritable—but she did remember that it enforced her belief that the nose of a German shepherd was remarkable . . . whether young or old . . . whether male or female . . . whether born in a large litter or a small litter.

"Do you really have a world-class nose, Bozo?" she asked. "Or do you just like socks?"

Upon hearing those words, Bozo paused in his sock manipulations and considered what he'd just heard. But he obviously considered it of no importance, because he went right back to the sock.

Didi pulled the door open and said: "Let's go for a walk, Bozo!" She stepped out into the hallway. Like a flash, Bozo left his sock and bolted out after her.

The moment he was outside, she stepped back inside, deft as a matador, and slammed the door shut.

She walked across the room, picked up the soiled black sock, and put it back in the carryall.

Bozo was crying piteously outside the door, heartbroken over having been hoodwinked.

Didi bent to untie her shoe. She then removed one of her own socks. Then she closed the carryall three-quarters shut.

She opened the door. Bozo bounded in.

Didi waved her sock at him.

Bozo leaped up, grabbed the sock out of her grasp, and rushed triumphantly back to his corner.

He flopped down and started to worry Didi's sock. But he didn't keep at it for long. It was obviously not to his liking.

Bozo glared accusingly at her. Then he plopped his face on his paws and started to snooze. But Didi could see that it was a fake snooze. He was watching her . . . oh yes . . . young Bozo was watching her.

She turned around and walked out of the room, closing the door authoritatively behind her.

She waited. She heard nothing. She waited. Then she heard sounds. She heard Bozo growling. She heard something being ripped and dragged.

Then all was silent.

She walked back into the room.

The carryall was in one corner of the room, ripped open, its contents strewn about.

The pup was in the other corner, absolutely luxuriating in the scent and texture of Mary Hyndman's old sock.

Didi stood watching him for a long time. "Little Bozo," she said to him, "when you open a can of worms, it stays open."

Chapter 12

Didi knew she was going too fast as she wheeled the red jeep into the state police barracks parking lot. Her rear right tire hit one of the concrete abutments and the other three tires screeched. But she came safely to a stop.

She was delighted to see Allie Voegler walking toward her from his own car.

"What's your hurry?" he asked angrily, approaching the jeep.

Then he saw the bruise on her face.

"Didi? Are you okay?"

"I fell," she explained. Then quickly she added: "I appreciate your coming again. I didn't expect you this early."

"You can't see Abigail until eight," Allie announced.

Didi climbed out of the jeep.

"There's one of those coffee trucks that pulls up about a hundred yards from here. Let's take a walk." He offered his arm in a rather absurdly gallant gesture given the time and the place. She took it and they walked slowly toward the road.

"I have some news for you," Allie said.

"Good news, I hope. I'm getting weary of the other kind."

"Brother Neil, according to the state troopers, has the kind of past you wouldn't have expected from a monk."

"Like what?"

"Bank embezzler. His real name was Vernon Monday. A real smooth operator. Gift of gab. He was born and raised in Lexington, Virginia. He worked in a bank in Charlotte, North Carolina, embezzled about eleven thousand dollars, was caught, convicted, and sentenced."

"What years?" Didi asked.

"Late seventies. But that's not all. He served three years at one of those federal minimum-security work camps and then just walked away with only eight months left on his sentence. Bizarre. So Brother Neil was, when you discount for everything, an escaped felon."

Didi didn't say a word.

"Well, what do you think of that?" Allie was visibly put out that his revelation had not elicited surprise from Didi.

"I kind of expected that," she finally replied.

"Oh, is that right?" he asked sarcastically.

They kept walking. She held his arm tighter.

"And I have some information for you," she said. "I found the puppy."

Allie stopped. "What puppy?" he asked. Then he laughed. "Oh, you mean Mary Hyndman's mythical puppy."

"Not mythical, Allie. I found the puppy at Alsatian House. He's adorable and he slept at the foot of my bed."

Allie seemed confused. "You mean Mary had adopted an Alsatian House shepherd?"

"Exactly."

"But how did it get back to the monastery? It's a long walk for a puppy, Didi."

"So it is."

"And why would they give out one of their puppies for adoption to a lady who could barely walk?"

"I don't know."

"Are you sure the dog was Mary's?"

"Allie, the most honest thing on earth is a German shepherd's nose."

"The wisdom of that escapes me."

They reached the mobile coffee hut. Allie purchased two coffees and one plain cruller, which he fastidiously broke in two equal parts. They stood by the side of the road like two adult waifs—the plainclothes Hillsbrook police officer and the vet.

When she had finished her half of the cruller, Didi asked: "When you told me that Abigail had been working for Mary Hyndman, did you think there was any connection between the two murders?"

"I learned about Abigail and Mary before Brother Neil was murdered."

"Okay, Allie, what about now? Do you think there is a connection now? Now that I have found Mary's puppy?"

"I don't know. The whole thing is bizarre."

"I don't like the word bizarre. It's frightening, Allie. Very, very frightening."

"Do you want another donut?" he asked.

"No. But I want you to sit in when I speak to Abigail."

"My pleasure," he said.

The shock had worn off. Abigail knew why she was locked up. She seemed to understand the gravity of her situation. She couldn't sit still in the small interrogation room. Didi noticed her pallor and her panic. Didi noticed that there were no belts or shoelaces or buckles or anything on her person that could even remotely be thought of as a suicide aide. Abigail was only a few years younger than she, but Didi looked upon her now as a child, a sad child in great trouble. She wanted to comfort her but she wasn't there for comfort that morning.

"You know what I miss most?" Abigail asked, her slender fingers spread out in a gesture of supplication.

Didi could never have guessed, so she didn't try.

Abigail answered her own question. "I miss Mrs. Tunney's oatmeal." The tears welled up in her eyes. Didi fought back tears also.

Abigail folded her arms, almost defiantly. "But I also miss Charlie and Trent Tucker and my hogs . . . and I miss you."

"Sit down, Abigail," Didi said softly. Abigail stared at her, then at Allie, who was standing quietly against one wall, then she sat down next to a bare table.

"Abigail," Didi said, "I know that you were working for Mary Hyndman."

The thrust of Didi's statement confused the

girl. She was obviously expecting something
about her situation now.

Abigail ignored the statement. She asked
Didi: "They're not going to let me out of here,
are they?"

"Not right now," Didi agreed. "But let's con-
centrate on Mary Hyndman for the moment.
You did work for her, didn't you?"

"Yes, yes, I did. I'm sorry I didn't tell you.
But Charlie told me to keep quiet. He said you
would be mad. He said you would complain
that we were not taking care of the house and
the property like we were supposed to . . . so
how could I have the time to help Mary."

"Why did you stop working for her?"

"It was a silly thing. I used to clean up for
her. And I used to play the radio when I
cleaned. She didn't like the music. She didn't
like what I played. So we had a fight. It wasn't
a bad fight. But she told me not to come
back."

It was the longest speech Didi had ever
heard Abigail make.

"Did Mary have a puppy, Abigail?"

"No. All her dogs had died."

Didi reached over and took her hand. "Abigail, you do know that I am your friend?"

"Yes! Yes!" Abigail said. "I loved your
mother. And I love you."

"I want to ask you an important question,
Abigail. I want you to give me a true answer."

"Yes. I won't lie to you."

Didi let go of the girl's hand and sat back.

"Did you know Brother Neil before we came
to Alsatian House?"

Abigail jerked both her hands off the table and tugged viciously at her long golden hair. Didi looked quickly at Allie, whose face registered perplexity and confusion.

Abigail did not answer. She started to shift in her seat.

"Tell me the truth, Abigail," Didi insisted.

"Yes," she finally said, very quietly. She seemed to slump over the table.

"Where did you meet him?"

"At Mary Hyndman's house."

"How many times did you see him?"

"Twice."

"What was he doing there?"

"I don't know."

"Did you know he was a monk?"

"Yes."

"Did you know he came from Alsatian House?"

"Yes."

"Did he talk about placing a puppy with Mary?"

"No."

"Did you like him?"

"Very much."

"And that's why you were happy when I took you along instead of Charlie?"

"Yes."

"Thank you, Abigail," Didi said. She stood up, leaning over the table and kissed her on the head.

"What next?" Allie asked. They were standing in front of her red jeep in the parking lot behind the state police barracks. It had turned into a brilliant summer morning.

"I kept seeing Mary hung up on that fence," Didi whispered. "As I was talking to Abigail that memory kept coming back."

"What next, Didi?" Allie persisted.

"Do you have a pad and pencil?"

Allie produced both. Didi opened the pad, rested it on the jeep's fender, and wrote a list of names: Brother Thomas. Brother Anthony. Sister Ruth. Sister Pia. Brother Samuel. Brother Lawrence.

Then she handed the notebook back to Allie. "Can you do a background check on these people?"

Allie grinned. "Do you think they're all embezzlers like Brother Neil? With warrants out for them."

When Didi didn't reply, Allie said: "Okay. I'll do the best I can. But I need the state troopers for this. Columbia County isn't my jurisdiction."

"No, Allie, but Mary Hyndman *is* your jurisdiction. And she was my mother's friend. And even if she hadn't been, she didn't deserve to die like that."

"Fine. No problem."

"And there's something else I want you to do."

"What's that?"

"Hover around."

Allie grinned. "Helicopters hover. Hummingbirds hover. Honeybees hover. Cops don't."

Didi climbed back into the seat.

"Where are you going now, Doctor N?"

"I am going to check back into the monastery."

"I didn't know you had checked out," Allie replied.

"Brother Thomas asked me to leave. He firmly believed my presence had opened the floodgates of sexual promiscuity in his garden."

"Obviously there's a side of you that I'm not familiar with," Allie noted. Then he asked: "If he doesn't want you there . . . how are you going to get back in?"

Didi smiled and turned the ignition key. The jeep turned over immediately. She said: "I'm going to do something very dishonest. I'm going to use my prestige as a veterinarian to construct a malicious lie and a fictitious danger."

"I don't have the slightest idea what you're talking about, Didi," Allie said.

"Just hover," she said, smiling, and started to pull away.

"Wait, Didi!" Allie called out. She braked. "How did you know that Abigail had met Brother Neil at Mary's?"

"One of those rare occasions when my feminine intuition is worth anything in the real world," Didi answered and drove off.

Chapter 13

Didi stood, outwardly calm, in front of the wicker desk. Brother Thomas sat facing her, his hands folded.

But Didi's surface calmness hid her inner turmoil . . . and shame. Yes, shame. She was about to misrepresent something . . . something that should never be misrepresented. Something that went to the very center of her being: her work.

"I thought you had left us," Brother Thomas said softly.

What price virtue? Didi thought. What price honesty? Two dead humans. One her mother's friend. One a stranger. And Abigail in prison.

"I had left, Brother Thomas, but I decided to come back because of my conscience. Even though you don't want me here."

"What is the matter with your conscience?"

"Agatha."

"She seems well now. And we are most grateful to you."

"I may have been mistaken about the puppies," Didi said.

"They *were* dead, weren't they?"

"Yes. But I didn't have time to examine them. They may not have been born dead."

"Then what killed them?"

"A parasite called N caninum. It causes a protozoal infection—neosporosis. It mostly affects litters. It can be transmitted transplacentally. It causes ascending paralysis of limbs . . . then rigid contractions . . . then death."

"How do you know?" asked Brother Thomas, the fear evident on his face.

"You take blood and other tests. But that's why I came back. If it was indeed N caninum, all your subsequent litters are at risk."

"What happens if they are infected? I mean the bitches."

"There are several modes of treatment."

Didi turned her face away. Everything she had told him was a damn lie except for the fact that a parasite named N caninum did kill litters.

Brother Thomas bowed his head onto the desk. Then he raised it and said: "You have taught me a lesson in humility."

"How so?"

"I drove you from here with bad manners. Yet you ignored the insults when you believed the dogs were in danger. Blessed are the single-hearted, for they shall see God."

Didi smiled at the quote from Matthew. She shot back with a quote her mother used to use, often ad nauseam. "I tell you, there will be more joy in heaven over one repentant sinner than over ninety-nine righteous people who have no need to repent."

"You are an uncommon young woman, Dr. Nightingale," Brother Thomas affirmed.

"And you are an uncommon Keeper of the Spirit," Didi replied with one of those strange inflections that would lead a neutral observer to suspect some sarcasm.

"Is there any way I can help? Or anyone here? We are all at your service, Dr. Nightingale. And in your debt."

"I need to look at the records first."

"Records? We are seldom visited by veterinarians. Our dogs are seldom in need of them."

"Not veterinary records. I need placement records. Where the adopted puppies were raised. Who their owners are. I want to contact them."

"Yes, of course. We have them. Brother Lawrence and Sister Ruth are in charge." He rang a large cowbell on his desk, then apologized to Didi for its use. "They gave it to me to save my strength. I rarely use it."

Brother Anthony appeared.

"Tell Brother Lawrence and Sister Ruth that Dr. Nightingale has come back to vet the dogs. It is an urgent matter. Tell them she is waiting here to see the placement records."

Brother Anthony moved quickly to follow Brother Thomas's bidding.

"He seems so efficient," Brother Thomas remarked of Brother Anthony, "but sometimes his synapses get crossed." He laughed at his own imagery. Then he said to Didi: "I must get down to the fields. I will leave you here."

He came over to her and shook her hand

firmly. "Please send my love to your young friend in prison. I do not judge."

"I will pass that on to Abigail," Didi replied.

Brother Thomas left the room. Didi felt a sudden rush of pride. It had been relatively easy—the lies. And she had succeeded beyond her wildest dreams.

She was going to get the adoption records. The puppy and Mary Hyndman were about to be joined. Once that was accomplished, she could trace their relationship back in time. She could bring Mary and Brother Neil and Bozo into some sort of coherent picture.

She walked to the enormous window. Allie's car was in the lot. Yes, he was hovering. She slipped out of the house and ran to the car.

"Did they welcome you back?" Allie asked.

"With love," she said breathlessly. "I can't stay, Allie. But can you be back about three o'clock? I might have some very important facts."

"Three it is," he agreed.

Didi ran back to Brother Thomas's office and paced the room.

She heard a sound in the hall. She peered out, looking for Brother Lawrence and Sister Ruth.

It was neither. It was Bozo.

He launched himself from about three feet away and almost knocked her down. His slobbering tongue washed her face down.

"Calm down, dopey. Calm down. I'm happy to see you, too. But I was away only a few hours."

Bozo sat down on his haunches, happy and panting.

She looked at him critically. He was going to be a humongous dog. His chest was deep.

"You were there, weren't you, Bozo? You were that mysterious puppy. Weren't you?"

He cocked his head and pointed his ears.

"You know what's going on here, don't you, Bozo?"

He groaned.

"But you won't talk. Who are you protecting, Bozo? Do you know who murdered Brother Neil?"

Didi suddenly felt stupid. Her questions seemed no longer to be playful. As if she really believed that German shepherds were that intelligent. There had been one Shepherd bitch, in a research lab at Columbia University, in the 1950s, who, according to the report, understood 1,200 voice commands and/or words. But this was Bozo.

"You wanted us?" Sister Ruth called out, standing in the doorway. Behind her was Brother Lawrence.

Bozo decided to move on, nipping playfully at Sister Ruth as he exited.

"Yes. I am going to examine all your dogs, and I need information on those puppies already placed."

"Well," Sister Ruth said, "that is readily available on the second floor. In fact the records room is the only open part of the second floor. We try to keep the second and third floors of the house closed off—otherwise heating it would be prohibitive."

"What are you looking for?" Brother Lawrence asked.

"Information."

"What kind of information?"

"Age of puppy when placed. Where placed. Any illnesses before or after placement. Inoculations. Standard stuff."

"Do you really believe there's an infection going around?" Sister Ruth asked. Her tone was mildly skeptical.

Didi smiled and did not respond to that question. She asked in return: "Will one of you show me to the records room now?"

They both turned and walked away. Didi followed them. Together they climbed a row of steep stairs off the hallway, and opened a very rickety door.

"It's the first room on the right. Every other room is closed tight."

The three of them entered the records room. There was no electricity; only two large battery-operated lanterns to cut the gloom.

A single long carpenter's table was in the center. No other furniture. On the table were two old-fashioned cardboard index card files.

Sister Ruth pushed one of the files toward Didi. "Help yourself," she said.

Didi began to go through the cards one by one.

The information on each card was uniform and clearly recorded with an old-fashioned fountain pen.

Name of person adopting

Address and telephone number

Profession, if any, and size of family

Whether any other pets are in household; if so, what
Sex and date of birth of puppy
Size and composition of litter
Coat color
Name of mother and father
Inoculations
Date puppy picked up
Communications between adopter and Alsatian House after puppy left the monastery.

On the bottom of many of the cards was the amount of money the person had donated to Alsatian House—before, at the time of, and subsequent to the adoption.

"He has a beautiful hand, doesn't he?" Sister Ruth asked.

"Who?"

"Brother Anthony. He took over the transcription of the information onto the cards after Brother Thomas's arthritis worsened."

"Yes. It is a beautiful handwriting," Didi agreed.

She moved slowly and methodically through the cards. At first she thought there was no order at all—they surely weren't filed alphabetically by name of the adopting person. But then she realized there was an arrangement— by date of adoption. The latest adoptions were in front—then going back in time.

Didi felt a growing panic as the cards flipped by.

There was no chair in the room, so her back ached from bending over the table.

And then she turned the last card over and straightened up.

No Mary Hyndman! No card for Mary Hyndman! No mention of Mary Hyndman! Everything was tumbling down.

"What's in this file?" she asked angrily, pointing to the second one.

"Nothing that would interest you," replied an obviously impatient Brother Lawrence.

"You'd be surprised what interests veterinarians," Didi replied.

"It's a file containing names of people who wish to adopt but for whom a puppy is not yet available," Sister Ruth explained.

"Where do you get the names?"

"They write to us. We write back telling them no puppy is available at present. Then we put their names on file and they wait."

"Then you have their letters?" Didi asked.

"No. We destroy them after their names are filed."

"Why?"

"I don't know. It's the way we do things," Sister Ruth answered testily.

Quickly, Didi thumbed through the waiting list once. Then she did it a second time, much more slowly.

No mention of Mary Hyndman.

She pushed the two files toward the center of the table.

"If you need access to this information again . . . or you want to contact someone who adopted a puppy . . . just ask Brother Lawrence or myself. We will be happy to take you here again."

They seemed to be in a great hurry to leave, to be out of there. Didi was in no such hurry.

Everything was wrong with their paperwork procedures and with their filing system. But it could have simply been impatience or lack of experience or saintliness. Very few monks are tolerable bureaucrats.

She had no reason to ask the next question . . . but she was curious.

"Where do you keep the dogs' papers?"

"What papers?"

"You know—breeding papers. American Kennel Club registrations, lineages; the usual papers required for purebred litters."

Sister Ruth smiled: "Our dogs have no papers."

Didi couldn't believe what she was hearing. "Are you serious?"

"Of course I'm serious," Sister Ruth affirmed. "We do not register any of our dogs with the American Kennel Club. We do not register any of our animals with breed associations. We do not provide family trees or lines of descent to anyone—they don't exist. And why would anyone need them? We aren't breeding show dogs."

Didi retorted angrily, "That's nonsense. It has nothing to do with whether you're breeding for show or not. What happens if the person you place the dog with wants to sell him or breed him? Proof of ownership and breeding is absolutely necessary."

Sister Ruth shook her head sadly. "You seem unable to understand what we are doing at Alsatian House."

"You treat us like we were a puppy mill," Brother Lawrence said bitterly.

"You misunderstand me," Didi said.

"I think Brother Lawrence is right," Sister Ruth countered. "You *are* dealing with us like we're a puppy mill. Now you and I know, *Doctor* Nightingale, that many puppy mills are quite clean and well run. What makes a kennel into a puppy mill is that they are breeding as many dogs as possible for profit in as short a space of time as possible. So they don't have the time or inclination to follow around laws of breeding. They don't, for example, give a damn about the Hardy-Weinberg Law. You *do* know what that is, don't you, Dr. Nightingale?"

"Vaguely."

"Well, let me refresh your memory. It's a very old law and it states that gene frequencies will remain more or less stable if your breeding population is large, if you encourage random mating, and if there is neither selection nor migration nor mutation."

"Listen, Sister Ruth, you are—"

Sister Ruth interrupted Didi's response. "And puppy mills don't follow that equally hoary old adage—'inbreed for three generations, outbreed for one.' But we do."

"I didn't know you outcrossed," Didi said.

"Not only do we import a German or Swedish dog every so often, but we don't bring one in based on color or height or conformation. We outcross with a *Schutzhund*."

Didi was impressed. She was familiar with the *Schutzhund* qualification, which originated in Germany and which meant a dog was proficient in Tracking, Obedience, Man-work, and Character.

But she didn't get a chance to compliment them. Sister Ruth and Brother Lawrence wheeled on a dime and walked away.

Didi followed them out of the room and down the steps.

"If you need any assistance in examining the dogs, or rounding them up, please tell me," said Sister Ruth, her tone softening.

"Not at this time," Didi replied. They left her there, in the hallway.

Didi walked slowly back to the room she had occupied. Bozo was inside, chewing contentedly in one corner on Mary Hyndman's sock. Didi closed the door and lay down on the narrow bed.

She was disgusted. Her lies had been for naught. There seemed to be no connection. And without connection, there would be no resolution. Mary Hyndman's murder would fade away . . . waiting for some chance event in the future when a redheaded man would crawl out of the woodwork a thousand miles away and confess to a cellmate or a bar companion who would then retell the confession to a police officer. It could be years. It could be never. And Abigail would rot away in some women's prison.

A chill went through her. What if Abigail had, indeed, shot Brother Neil. Abigail *was* a very strange girl. What if she *had* murdered him? And if the same weapon that murdered Brother Neil turns out to be the same weapon that murdered Mary Hyndman—was it possible that Abigail had also shot the old woman? They had fought over something stupid. Perhaps the ethereal Abigail was really a demonic angel. Perhaps she was one of those strange creatures who could sing "Amazing Grace" with uncommon beauty and then calmly pull a trigger.

Didi sat up quickly. These thoughts were poisonous. And ridiculous. She stared at Bozo. "Are you lying to me, Bozo? Is that it? Maybe you have no idea that sock is Mary's. Maybe you were not her puppy. Maybe you're just a crazed sock fiend and that one in particular turns you on." Bozo paid no attention to the fact that his veracity was being maligned.

Didi stared glumly at the sock. Stupid, pathetic sock. She remembered how sad she felt when the druggist gave it to her . . . asking her to deliver it to Alsatian House. Poor Mary Hyndman's last request—a bunch of crushed bills totaling just a little more than a hundred dollars.

It had been sad then and it was sad now.

For the first time in Alsatian House, Didi felt very alone and very insecure. She needed a friend. She needed some of Brother Thomas's "Spirit" . . . whatever and whoever that may be.

She had the almost delicious feeling that she ought to pray. To the Spirit. Her mother had always prayed. But to a specific Father, Son, and Holy Ghost. Her father, she had heard, prayed constantly to his Protestant Jehovah.

Did poor old Mary pray before she was murdered?

She grimaced. Why was she always thinking

of Mary Hyndman with the phrase "poor old Mary"?

As if Mary Hyndman was some kind of old biddy who had always elicited sympathy. That was not what Mary Hyndman was about. She was a very tough woman . . . physically tough . . . intellectually tough . . . even in old age. She had never, never elicited sympathy . . . only admiration. People sought her out to be comforted or enlightened . . . not to bring comfort or enlightenment to her . . . and certainly not out of pity.

Didi stared at the mangled sock lying near Bozo.

She stood up, suddenly.

Yes, she thought, that was the problem with that damn sock and its pathetic contents. Saving those pathetic crumpled one-dollar bills. It was something an old biddy would do.

It surely was *not* what Mary Hyndman would do. It was not in character at all.

She walked over to the sock. Bozo started playing "protect the sock" and nipped at her boots.

But why would Mary do something so out of character?

Didi walked back to the bed and sat down. Why? Why? Why?

What if, she thought, it was some kind of message from Mary Hyndman to the monks at Alsatian House?

What if, she thought, it was decidedly *not* a message of love?

She sprang up from the bed, her entire body tensed. A terrible scenario suddenly presented itself to her. "Oh my!" she said out loud. Then she sat back down and tried to deal with it.

Allie was on time as usual. Didi slipped into the front seat beside him.

"Got anything?" he asked.

"According to the monastery records, there is no connection with Mary Hyndman," Didi replied.

"Then we were barking up the wrong tree?"

"No. Right tree, wrong bark."

"What does that mean?"

Didi changed the subject. She didn't want to tell him what she was thinking but she needed him to play out what she was thinking. One had to tread carefully with Allie Voegler, she knew. He was very quick to take affront. Often, over things that no one would pay attention to. It was, she realized, to some extent his feeling for her.

"Could you find any background information on those names?"

"Not yet. It's going to take time on that, Didi."

"What's going on in Hillsbrook?" she asked.

"Well, people heard about Abigail. They can't believe it."

They sat in silence for a while. The car windows were wide open. A bee kept darting in and out across the front window.

"You look pale, Didi," he noted.

"You mean my beauty has gone?" she asked sardonically.

He turned in his seat and pulled her close to him, trying to kiss her. She fought loose with a fury. "What the hell is the matter with you, Allie?"

He stormed out of the unmarked police car and sulked for a while. Then he appeared at the window: "I'm sorry. I'm really sorry. It's just that it has been so long since we've been close to each other . . . I mean . . . physically close."

Didi thought: What is this man talking about? We never slept together. Does he mean just sitting quietly together in the front seat of a car? These men in the country towns, Didi thought, are so strange. She, like Allie, had been raised in dairy farm country, although Allie had lived in the village. But Didi's sojourn in the big city for many years had shown her that a more sophisticated male was extant. It was only after she returned to Hillsbrook that she began to miss the men in Philadelphia. One needs a certain level of sophistication to make life bearable, otherwise one was always being grabbed in front seats. Not sophistication of motives . . . just behavior. She had no illusion about big-city men.

Didi laughed out loud at her train of thoughts. The pot was boiling. She had one last chance to extricate Abigail. She had one ferocious hunch that was wild but perhaps true. She had one final plan that might . . . it just might work. And here she was, waxing philosophical on the merits of men relative to their geography just because some fool had tried to kiss her.

"Allie, do me a favor and get back in the car. I have to talk to you."

Allie Voegler, holding his big frame in a kind of apologetic question mark, slipped back into the seat. Didi could see that his shirt was drenched through with sweat.

"Did you notice any farm stands around here?" she asked.

"Farm stands." He repeated and then seemed to be thinking. "Sure, there's all kinds of farm stands around here, Didi. One just down the road. They have squash and tomatoes and peppers."

"That'll be fine," Didi said.

"You mean you want me to drive you to a farm stand, now?"

"Yes. If you don't mind."

He started the engine, pulled out of the parking spot, and headed down the road at a very slow pace. They reached the first stand very quickly; a small makeshift shed right off the road. It consisted of two poles with a blanket over the top and the fruit and vegetables, in small baskets on folding tables. A young girl sat on the ground beside the stand, reading a book.

"Could you get me three tomatoes?" she asked Allie.

"Sure." He climbed out of the car and walked to the stand.

He came back a minute later without the tomatoes.

"What's the matter?" Didi asked.

"They only sell tomatoes by the basket."

"Okay, Allie. Buy the basket."

He left and returned shortly with the basket. Didi placed it on her lap and picked out three tomatoes. She then put the basket on the backseat.

"Why only three tomatoes?" Allie asked.

"Why not?"

Allie looked puzzled. He started to ask for an explanation, then thought better of it.

"Do you want to go back to Alsatian House now?" he asked.

"No. I want to talk to you for a minute, Allie."

"Go ahead. Talk."

"What are you doing tonight?"

"Probably sleeping," he replied.

"I have a proposition to make you," she said.

"I'm listening."

"If you are willing to stay up all night I'll put Mary Hyndman's murderer in your lap. And the murderer of Brother Neil."

"Gift wrapped?"

"Not exactly. But just be at Mary Hyndman's place around eight this evening. I'll meet you there."

"Are you serious?"

"Quite serious. Just park the car out of sight. I'll meet you behind her house."

"Do you know what you're doing, Didi? Or is this one of your crazy schemes?"

"I never knew I indulged in crazy schemes, Allie. People look upon me as a rather conservative vet. Young but conservative."

Allie started drumming on the wheel. He was obviously contemplating the offer, seriously. Finally, he asked: "What are you up to, Didi?"

"Let's just say I've changed my therapeutic approach."

"Speak English, huh!"

"Okay. Let me give you an instance. In the old days, when dairy farmers believed that there was a contagion in the herd, they didn't call a veterinarian. They merely moved the herd and shot those who couldn't travel. Oddly enough, it was a very good procedure. Primitive, brutal, but often successful in keeping a herd healthy and producing."

"Oh," Allie replied sardonically, "you're going to move the monks out of Alsatian House and those who can't leave are the sick ones. And by sick ones I assume you mean murderous ones."

"Not quite, Allie. Let's just say I'm going to give this particular herd of milking cows another piece of pasture to think about. Just think about."

"A therapeutic fantasy?"

"Sometimes you're brilliant, Allie."

Allie drummed harder on the wheel. "What do I have to lose? After all, it's what I always wanted—hours alone in a secluded spot with you."

Didi wandered about the grounds with an official-looking clipboard that she had requisitioned from Brother Thomas's crowded desk. She appeared to be examining German shepherds wherever she found them. She appeared to be making notes on her clipboard. She appeared to be taking blood and stool and tissue samples. But it was all fake. She was doing absolutely nothing except waiting for the evening meal.

At two minutes past six she entered the mess hall for the dinner meal, carrying only a small paper bag.

She waited patiently on line for servers to fill her tray—and fill it they did. There was turkey hash and creamed corn, stewed peaches and carrots glazed in honey. There was herbal tea and fresh apple juice.

She looked around.

At one table sat Brothers Samuel and Lawrence along with Sisters Pia and Ruth.

At a smaller table sat Brothers Thomas and Anthony.

She sat down at the larger table and they all immediately began to ask questions about what she had found in her examination, if anything.

The moment Brothers Thomas and Anthony saw her sit, they hurried to her table; Brother Anthony bringing up a chair for the older man.

"Did you find it?" Brother Thomas asked anxiously. "Did you find evidence of . . ." He had evidently forgotten the name of the infecting agent.

"N caninum," Didi helped him. Then she added: "It is too soon to tell. The labs have the final say."

"I think it's a false alarm," Sister Ruth said.

"From your lips to God's ears," said Brother Thomas.

Everyone began to eat, a bit nervously.

Didi seemed to be engrossed in her food, eating with gusto.

Suddenly she stopped eating and abruptly slammed her fork down on the table.

Everyone looked at her.

"I have a confession to make to you, Brother Thomas . . . to all of you."

They waited, curious, looking at each other.

"That money I brought you . . . that money in the sock . . . from the old woman who died . . . who asked me to bring it to you . . . do you remember that, Brother Thomas?"

"Yes I do," Brother Thomas affirmed vigorously.

"Well, that woman, Mary Hyndman, never gave me any money to give you. She gave me something else. And it just would have embarrassed me to give you it. So, I found an old sock in the trunk of my car and I stuffed it with all the bills Abigail and I had in our purses."

"But what did she mean Alsatian House to have?" Brother Thomas asked.

Didi picked up the paper bag that was nestled between her feet. She opened the bag and dumped the three tomatoes onto the table.

"Tomatoes?" Brother Thomas asked, touching one of them. There was laughter around the table.

"Oh, not these ones," Didi explained. "This Mary Hyndman, may she rest in peace, was a fine gardener. I got these at a farm stand down the road. Hers were better. But I had no other way to reproduce the gift."

Brother Thomas looked at her sternly. "It was silly of you to do that, Dr. Nightingale. We at Alsatian House appreciate all gifts equally."

Didi looked dreadfully apologetic. "I realize I

did a bad thing. I'm sorry. And I'm glad to get it off my chest."

Everybody nodded their approval and went back to the meal.

Good. That part of the plan had gone over well enough. But how much had they believed? How deep had the hook penetrated? It was too soon to tell.

Didi waited a few seconds. Then she picked up her knife and fork . . . but she didn't eat. For once, she was uninterested in the wonderful Alsatian House food.

Chapter 14

Allie was lounging against the small back porch of Mary Hyndman's house. The moment he saw Didi he grinned and said: "I was going to bring a butterfly net to get that redheaded fiend who you are going to drop in my lap tonight . . . but then I decided that I didn't have one with the required mesh size."

Didi didn't think it was funny; she was nervous, very nervous. And she had forgotten to wear her work boots.

"I brought a flashlight," she said.

"Good. Now tell me where and when this arrest is going to happen."

"If it happens it'll happen in the tomato patch."

"What tomato patch? I've been through her fields searching for that damn puppy. Remember? There isn't no tomato patch. It's all a jumble."

"You're unsophisticated, Allie," she noted, "in regards to how Mary gardened. She interfiled crops. She mixed them. Everything, according to her, is a companion plant."

"Like you and me?" he queried.

"What?"

"Well, aren't we companion plants?"

"I never thought of us in a horticultural mode," Didi commented. For some reason Allie found that very amusing.

"Then pick another mode," he said, "if you don't like that one. How about the frustration mode?"

"Can't we postpone this kind of conversation for a more appropriate setting?"

"As you wish, Dr. Nightingale," he replied, with the kind of deferential sarcasm that only cops seem to have perfected.

The air had grown damp. It was hot. A slight breeze was coming from the west. The gloom increased as the last rays of the dying sun petered out. She was frightened as well as nervous. But more for what might *not* happen. All her eggs, as they say, were now in one basket.

They circled the house and entered the garden area. They didn't have to worry about bruising growing things because Mary was dead; the garden had been abandoned.

Didi stopped when she felt Allie's hand on her back.

She turned. "What?" Her voice was a whisper.

"It suddenly dawned on me . . . those three tomatoes you took from the box."

"What about them?"

"Does it have something to do with why we're here?"

"Everything has something to do with everything else," she responded cryptically. Then she headed deeper into the garden.

It took them a full half hour of exhausted

meandering to find the sliver of tomato plants that wound its way in and out of a stand of corn.

How flimsy they seemed between the tall, sturdy stalks.

The name of an old movie popped into her head. *Crossover Dreams,* it had been called, if she remembered correctly. It was a movie about a Hispanic singer in New York City who was trying to cross over into the Anglo hit parade. Like a tomato plant trying to jump the border and get into the corn.

What a silly thing to remember, she thought. And then something else popped into her head. Not so silly. The name of her professorial lover from vet school, Drew Pelletier. This thought unnerved. Why was she thinking of him just now?

Was she somehow comparing him to Allie Voegler? Was that it? No. Not that. There was absolutely no comparison. She had never slept with Allie. Drew had been her first and only lover. He had broken the affair up and she was so desolated by the breakup that she had applied and gone to India to do field work on Asian elephants. No . . . there was no comparison in any way, shape, or form.

Then she remembered a single unimportant conversation. Drew and she, after they had made love in her small apartment, would stay together in that rickety bed for a long time. And for some reason what they always talked about after making loving was, as strange as it seems, veterinary medicine. Oh, they had many other kinds of conversations—about

eros and death and movies and clothes and
cities and country life—but after lovemaking it
was always about veterinary medicine.

One conversation had been about tomato
mites. She had seen an article that mites were
savaging tomato crops. Drew had started to
discourse about the importance of mites in
equine disease, which was his specialty. He
told her about the tropical fowl mite that is
hosted by chickens, pigeons, myna birds,
ducks, and man, to name just a few. Drew had
told her that western equine encephalomyeli-
tis virus had been recovered from that mite.

Didi cringed at the bizarre specificity of her
memory. Why had she recalled such a ridiculous conversation now? Get hold of yourself,
she commanded herself silently. Get hold!

"Now what do we do?" Allie asked, staring
at the tomato plants with disgust.

Didi looked around. It was dark now. A half
moon overhead. She felt very vulnerable. She
felt that it was bordering on the unbelievable
that she was in that garden at that time. She
felt a strong resentment against her tendency
to leap before she looked when faced with an
intellectual barrier.

"It is easier to reach this patch from the
front of the garden than from where we entered," she said.

She pointed across to a thick stand of corn.

"We'll wait there," she said.

Allie walked into the stand first. His large
body parted the corn.

"Far enough!" Didi called out. "We have to
stay close."

"To what?"

"The tomato patch."

There was no place to sit. They had to wait, standing.

The half moon kept vanishing and reappearing. A wet fog came and went and came again. They waited, standing, not more than two feet from each other; not more than five feet from the border of the tomato patch.

At ten o'clock a stiff Allie asked her: "Am I really going to be rich and famous after this?"

"Sure," Didi replied. "You'll probably win the Dutchess County Police Officer of the Year certificate."

"And you'll win a fifth prize for tomatoes at the Dutchess County Fair."

"And you'll win the first annual Ugliest Flannel Shirt award, given by the Hillsbrook Chamber of Commerce."

"And you'll win the first . . ."

On and on they bantered, the prizes getting uglier and more aggressive. Their voices were exaggerated whispers.

Then, as suddenly as the verbal joust had started, it ended. They stood quietly, a bit chastened. Didi realized she was only twenty yards away, if that, from where Mary Hyndman had been displayed—on the fence.

Didi shifted her weight from one foot to another. How many hours could she stand? She didn't know. She looked quickly at Allie. His face was cast in shadowy bronze. She didn't have to worry about him, she knew. Country macho, he would die standing rather than admit he wanted to—needed to—sit. Besides, there is no place to sit in a corn stand.

There was a slight stirring behind them. Allie tensed. It vanished. And then the sound came again—from a different direction. Very low, very persistent. A rustling.

"Did you hear it?" he asked.

"Field mice," she replied.

"How do you know?"

"Because it's their garden now."

"The owls will get some of them," Allie noted.

"And the feral cats."

"Do you like field mice, Didi?"

"I guess I do."

"Why do people like field mice and hate house mice?"

"I don't know."

"I find that very strange."

"Perhaps it's because field mice have tufted ears," Didi offered.

"Coyotes have tufted ears and most people don't like coyotes."

"I like coyotes," Didi said.

Then Allie left the subject of tufted ears and confessed that his most secret desire was to resign from the police force and move all the way upstate and live like a mountain man in the Adirondacks.

"You mean as a poacher?" Didi needled.

"No, as a vet," Allie shot back.

"Right. Allie Voegler, DVM. Have Winchester, will travel. You guarantee to solve tick problems. Shoot the dogs and shoot the deer."

"Not funny," Allie replied.

Why are we always fighting? Didi thought.

Every conversation, no matter how innocent, ends up vituperative. She shifted her weight again.

Suddenly she thought of poor Abigail, huddled in that miserable cell in Columbia County. There was no way to succor her.

She looked at her luminous dial. It was past midnight. Soon, she realized, it would have to be soon, if she had been right. If she had figured wrong, she could stand in that garden until Christmas.

Should she tell Allie *why* they were in that garden?

Why hadn't she told him? Was it only because her plan was so outlandish? Her reading of what had happened so foreign to a police officer? Her gamble such a long shot?

Or was it because deep down, she really didn't trust Allie Voegler?

Bozo had spent the early evening chasing something. He really didn't know what he was chasing, but if he would have caught it in the brush he would have snapped its neck with his strong puppy jaws and probably tried to eat it. Unless of course it had been a feral cat . . . in which case he would have gotten his beautiful nose bloody.

It was getting dark and Bozo did not like the dark. He went to the side of the mess tent where his mother was curled up, greeted her, and then gallumped off to the big house to sleep with his new friend.

The door to the room was a bit open. He pushed through. She wasn't there. He walked to the corner of the room and plopped down, exhausted from his hunting.

He caught the familiar odor near him and reached out, puppylike, to bring the sock to him . . . to chew it a bit.

But the sock wasn't there. He moved his head from side to side trying to locate it. It wasn't there. He got up and searched the room, even under the bed.

He reached the door and stared back into the room, angry at the betrayal. He sat for a moment. Then he moved outside the room and began to search. The odor was faint but there.

Brother Thomas was asleep at the desk when Bozo entered the office. His face was turned sideways over a pile of bills. One arm was stretched out on the wicker desk, the other arm in his lap.

Bozo stuck his head under the hand on the lap and shoved upward.

Brother Thomas woke suddenly—confused. He didn't know where he was or who he was. He stood up, in a panic. And then the stupefaction passed. He sat back down and for the first time noticed Bozo, who was seated and waiting for the old man to give him his sock.

"Hello," Brother Thomas said. Bozo started to whine.

"What are you doing at this hour?" he asked kindly.

Bozo approached him again, put both paws on the old man's lap, and pulled himself up so that he and the monk were face to face. Then he hugely licked the old man's face.

Brother Thomas hugged the puppy. He said

to him, with kindness and great affection: "Something is troubling you, my young pagan. What is it? Do you seek conversion?"

Bozo disengaged himself, ran off a few feet, then began to pace and moan.

"No conversion without instructions first," Brother Thomas said to him, with a bit of a giggle, waggling his finger at the puppy.

Bozo added a few deep-chested miserable moans, as if his stomach were being tortured.

"Or is it that you are hungry? That your brothers and sisters have taken your food?"

Bozo just collapsed onto the floor, with a look of hurt on his face . . . a look so pathetic that it was obvious to all the world that this puppy had been wronged.

"Maybe, just maybe, I can ease your distress," Brother Thomas said.

Darkness had already fallen. A single table light was on the desk. Brother Thomas stood up again, moved the lamp toward the edge of the table, turned, and began to look through the battered files on the window closest to the desk.

"Yes, I may have something for you, my friend. If I remember where I put it."

Then he stopped searching, stared for a moment at the puppy, and asked him: "Did you know that I almost became a 'whiskey priest'?"

Then he searched with renewed effort and finally pulled an object out with a triumphant "ah . . . Look here!"

Bozo looked and didn't move.

It was an old, well-chewed rawhide bone.

"Come on, friend. It's for you." Brother Thomas held it up and turned it around as if it were the most glorious and most succulent of objects.

Bozo approached it slowly, warily, making little detours as he moved in.

Brother Thomas kept his arm and the object in his hand very still.

Finally, Bozo reached the rawhide bone. He sniffed it, then turned half away as if he really didn't want it, then turned back and with a snap of his jaw plucked the rawhide bone out of the offering hand and began to prance triumphantly about the room. He had already forgotten about the sock.

Brother Thomas shut the light off and headed down the hallway for his evening ritual. He always said good night to his brothers and sisters. But not face to face. He had his own special way. Just a prayer.

He stopped in front of Brother Samuel's room. The door was closed but the light was on inside. Probably reading, Brother Thomas thought. Samuel loved to read fat books about explorers in Africa . . . about finding the source of the White Nile and the Blue Nile . . . about treks up Mount Kilamanjaro . . . about expeditions to primeval rain forests.

Brother Thomas closed his eyes and uttered a brief prayer for the soul of Brother Samuel, in this world and the next. Then he reflected on his friendship with Samuel and prayed to be worthy of it, for Samuel was a good and responsible man and one of the spiritual bulwarks of Alsatian House.

He moved to Sister Pia's room. The door was closed and the light on. Sister Pia liked to write letters at night. He closed his eyes and uttered a prayer for the soul of Sister Pia. He remembered her *joie de vivre*, her sense of fun. She was indispensable because she was so alive. He prayed that he could be worthy of her optimism.

He moved to Brother Lawrence's room. The door was shut. The light was out. He prayed for Brother Lawrence's soul . . . he prayed that this man whom the world had so wounded both physically and mentally would have peace in his life at Alsatian House.

Then he prayed in front of the door to Sister Ruth's room. He prayed for her and for himself . . . that he would have the strength to be worthy of her friendship, for she was the true Mistress of the Hounds . . . the woman who had brought the Alsatian House German Shepherds to such prominence.

He passed quickly by the room in which Brother Neil had lived and made the sign of the cross.

In front of Brother Anthony's room he clasped his hands and prayed very hard. Brother Anthony was but a child. He had a child's fervor without focus. But he would one day be a man of great empathy. Brother Thomas intuited that.

His nightly ritual concluded, he opened the door to his room. But he did not go inside. He stood there, poised. He had napped in his office and sleep was far from him now, he knew.

It would be best to have a walk . . . a long walk in the warm night.

He closed his door and walked back down the hall and out onto the great lawn. It was a cloudy night but the lawn sparkled with reflected light from the river below the bluff. Even if the moon and stars were totally obscured, the river and the banks of the river would have that strange illumination. Brother Thomas never knew what it was. He surmised that it came from the fact that the river was so absorbent. Like a white robe.

Clasping his hands behind his back, he walked around the big house and headed for the fields. The arthritis was starting to bother him, as it always did at night and in the morning. The fingers this time.

A cloud parted and Brother Thomas could see the half moon. He kept walking, slowly, watching the moon. He started to breathe deeply.

For the first time in several days he was beginning to feel good—healthy. Almost strong.

Yet, at the same time his fingers were hurting dreadfully. It was a mystery. How could one part of the body be so deformed even if it resides in a larger and more healthful whole?

The speculation unnerved him. It was not his task to speculate thusly. He remembered that passage from Corinthians:

You must know that your body is a temple of the Holy Spirit. Who is within? The Spirit you have received from God. You are not your own. You have been purchased, and at what a price! So glorify God in your body.

A man, he thought, could spent three lifetimes trying to live by that wisdom and another four lifetimes trying to understand it.

He stopped walking suddenly and looked around. This place he was standing on was familiar.

Very familiar!

He felt a sudden chill. He was standing on the exact spot of earth where Brother Neil was murdered.

Brother Thomas began to tremble. He had been walking randomly but the Spirit had led him to this spot. Yes, that was for sure.

He knew what it meant. He was next! He would die next!

Fear enveloped him. He didn't want to die yet! There was still much to do. Much to do. He fell to his knees and held his arms up in supplication.

"Please!" he cried out. "Give me time! Give me more time!"

He felt dizzy. He redoubled his cries but they grew weaker. He fell forward, onto his face.

"Brother Thomas! Brother Thomas!"

A hand was pulling at him, and then lifting him. He opened his eyes.

"I heard cries. What happened, Brother Thomas? What happened?" asked Sister Ruth as she cradled the old man in her arms.

"I don't know. I don't know!" Brother Thomas said. He looked hard into her sturdy face. "We are like a Pieta," he added.

Sister Ruth smiled. "Yes, you are fine," she said. "Come, grab hold, let us get you up."

She helped him to his feet. Six of the German shepherds had joined them. Like good shepherds everywhere, they used their bodies to keep him standing, for he was of their flock.

"I feel strong again," Brother Thomas said. He stared at the animals about him. They were so beautiful, so elegant.

"Let us go back to the house, Brother Thomas. You need rest."

He nodded. Sister Ruth took his arm and they started to walk slowly.

"Do you know the chariot?" he asked.

"No," replied Sister Ruth, perplexed.

"That blazing chariot that took Ezekiel to heaven . . . the chariot with wheels like golden scythes."

"Ah yes, *that* chariot."

"The chariot in which the prophets are brought to the right hand of God, Sister Ruth."

"Of course, Brother Thomas. Watch your step."

"Well, I will not need a chariot when it happens. I am not a prophet. Perhaps I am not even a man of God. But when I am called, Sister Ruth, I know how I shall ascend."

"How?"

"On the backs of our lovely dogs. They will bring me there. Like a wounded lamb. Eight, ten, twenty of them will carry me there. Yes, I know that."

"Watch your step."

They went into the house together—Brother

Thomas and Sister Ruth and the German shepherds.

Bozo, who was chewing his new toy in the hallway, just flicked his tail a few times in greeting. He couldn't be bothered with any social interaction.

Chapter 15

A beam of light cut through the corn stand and illuminated both humans and plants.

As fast as it appeared it was gone.

"What was that?" Didi whispered urgently.

"A car beam, coming off the road. Shh! Listen."

Yes, there was a car on Mary Hyndman's property. Didi heard a low, quiet throbbing. And then it was gone, like the beam of light.

"Turn the ignition off," Allie whispered.

Didi clutched the flashlight tightly. She stood absolutely straight up, still, like a cornstalk. Allie bent down gingerly and pulled the weapon from his ankle holster. Then he stood straight . . . like Didi, in an exaggerated posture.

They heard nothing for five paralyzing minutes. And then the soft slow crutch of footsteps in the garden. They seemed far, far away.

Didi dropped her head and closed her eyes. The excitement, the anticipation, the fear made her woozy. She shook her head. The wooziness vanished. The hand that held the flashlight was damp from sweat. She moved it to the other hand.

Now the crunching steps were closer, much closer. For the first time she sensed mosquitos or blow flies about her face.

The steps ceased.

A minute later a dull thud. Then another one. It is a shovel, she thought. A shovel! Allie touched her arm. He pointed to the left side of the stand. He shook his head.

The intruder, Didi realized, was only a few feet away, digging in that meandering tomato patch.

Allie pointed to her flash. She nodded. He gave her a thumbs-up sign.

Then he screamed out "NOW!" And leapt past her, trampling the corn. Didi flicked the light on and followed as fast as she could.

"Don't move! Don't move! Stay! Hands up! Don't move!"

Her flashlight illuminated Allie, who was in a standing crouch, screaming at the intruder, holding the weapon straight out. The effect was paralyzing.

Didi shone the light on the intruder who stood, trembling, hands held high, a shovel leaning against his leg.

Allie moved closer and kicked the shovel away.

It wasn't the redheaded bogus doctor. It was young Brother Anthony.

"Can I put my hands down?" he asked quietly. He seemed to be recovering quickly from the shock.

Didi knew she would have to break him fast.

She gathered her strength, breathing in and out quickly.

"What were you digging for?" Allie asked.

Brother Anthony didn't answer. "The tomatoes are not ripe yet," Allie said, circling him and running his hands up and down Brother Anthony's body to look for weapons. "Besides," he added, "you pick tomatoes with your hands. You don't dig with a shovel. Or are you a city boy?"

Allie stepped back but kept his weapon cocked and high.

Yes, Didi thought, she would have to break him now, right here in the tomato patch, or perhaps never.

"Take him in, Allie! He murdered Mary Hyndman! The redheaded man was just a decoy. He drove out the front way after Brother Anthony had murdered Mary. Brother Anthony took the puppy and left through the far field. It was perfectly planned."

Brother Anthony's eyes went furiously from Didi to Allie. He didn't say a word.

"Take him in, Allie! He murdered Mary!"

Brother Anthony said: "I never even met Mary Hyndman."

Didi shouted: "Take him in, Allie. Show him no mercy! He didn't show Mary any!"

Allie pulled a pair of handcuffs from his back pocket.

Brother Anthony cringed at the sight of the silvery manacles.

Didi caught his fear. She watched his eyes grow wide. The fear of being manacled! Like a beautiful young filly who would destroy herself against the walls of her stall rather than be roped.

"Put them on him, Allie," she yelled.

Brother Anthony folded his arms across his chest in a prayerful gesture. The fear of the manacles seemed to crumble his body. "Please, don't," he begged.

Allie stopped moving toward him.

Brother Anthony said, a loud, quavering voice: "I didn't kill that old woman. And there is no redheaded man. That was Brother Samuel with a wig. I wasn't with him. I never knew he would kill her."

"Who else was involved?"

"No one. Brother Samuel ran the whole thing."

"What whole thing?"

Brother Anthony was having trouble breathing. He held up his hand asking for time.

"What thing?" Didi demanded.

Brother Anthony recovered his breath. "Alsatian House is a dying institution. Brother Thomas could never raise enough money. We owe hundreds of thousands of dollars in taxes and interest payments. Brother Samuel found a way to keep us going and he forced Brother Neil and myself to work with him. I had no choice."

"Why didn't you have a choice?"

"Because five years ago I pleaded guilty to perjuring myself at a trial. I was supposed to show up for sentencing. Instead I ran. To Alsatian House. Brother Samuel found out. He threatened me with disclosure. Oh, Brother Thomas wouldn't have cared. He accepts everyone. He provided sanctuary for everyone. But the county police and the state troopers would have cared. They would have taken me away."

"It was extortion, wasn't it?" Didi demanded. "That wonderful plan of Brother Samuel to save Alsatian House was extortion and worse."

"Yes, it was. We never used to place puppies with old ladies who lived alone. But then Brother Samuel decided to do it. To give puppies to old women who he thought had money. After a certain period of time, when they had become attached to the puppy, we threatened to remove the dog unless we were given money."

"You people make pimps and drug dealers look like the Archangel Michael," Allie interjected. Didi held out one hand, signaling that he shouldn't interfere right now.

"Why did Brother Samuel need you and Brother Neil?" she asked.

"I was the one who opened and read the correspondence from people who wanted puppies. I isolated the promising ones, gave them to Brother Samuel, and he took it from there. If a puppy was placed with an old woman, I would write out a different name on the record. That way, all the dogs were accounted for. No one ever really checked the names on the card with the people who adopted. I destroyed all the correspondence. That's why he needed me."

"And Brother Neil?"

"Brother Neil delivered the puppies and

picked them up. He was the one who closed the trap on the old ladies."

"Then he took the puppy from Mary Hyndman?"

"Yes. She claimed she had money. But she refused to give it to us. She begged to keep the puppy anyway. No go. When Brother Neil took the puppy from her, she went kind of crazy. She threatened to call the police . . . the newspapers . . . the television stations. Brother Neil told Brother Samuel. He murdered her."

"And why did he murder Brother Neil?"

"Brother Neil was going to tell Brother Thomas what was going on . . . how his beloved monastery was currently being financed. Brother Samuel shot him in the head. He left the weapon on the ground beside the body. Your young friend, the girl, was stupid enough to pick it up."

Didi felt her body collapsing from weariness and from the sheer weight of the ugliness she was hearing. She walked over to the shovel and touched it with the point of her foot.

"What were you digging up, Brother Anthony?" she asked.

Brother Anthony shook his head. "I don't know. Maybe money. The old woman's secret cache. Maybe a tape recording of herself being extorted. Brother Samuel didn't know. But he thought I should look. Because of those tomatoes you said were Mrs. Hyndman's real gift to us. It was just the kind of cryptic message that old woman would send. She was a gardener, wasn't she? She grew tomatoes. Maybe she had changed her mind before that last visit

with her . . . maybe she was going to give us
the money to keep the puppy . . . maybe she
had left some kind of message to that effect.
We just didn't know. But Brother Samuel told
me to dig up her tomato patch. When you first
came to the monastery, Brother Samuel was
suspicious. Because he told me that you had
passed him on the road that day, and had
words. But you never recognized him. And you
seemed to be just a friend of Mary's, doing a
good deed. And then, when you were brave
enough to admit you had destroyed her real
gift to us . . . tomatoes . . . Brother Samuel
told me I must come here."

"It was a lie, Brother Anthony."

"What was a lie?"

"The tomatoes. Mary Hyndman never gave
anyone any tomatoes to bring to you. She gave
a dirty sock full of crumpled bills to her druggist and asked him to get it to Alsatian House
if she died. Or, perhaps, if she was murdered.
It was a gift of hate for you. It was Mary's way
of telling you that you and all your prayers
and singing were ultimately about dirty money
hidden in dirty socks."

"Did she have money hidden away?"

"I haven't the slightest idea."

"If she did have money, would she hide it
there . . . in the garden?" he pressed. He
seemed to have forgotten that he had been
part of a murderous plot. He was asking the
kinds of questions that only the innocent ask.

"I don't know."

Didi picked up the shovel, dropped the
flashlight, and impaled the spade into the

earth. She looked around. The patch needed weeding. She wondered if Bozo had joined Mary in the garden while she weeded. How Mary must have loved him! Didi knelt down and began to cry.

Allie picked up the flash, focused it on Brother Anthony's face, and kept it there.

Didi wiped the tears away savagely and stared at the young monk. He was, in fact, the only one she had seen at Alsatian House who looked like a monk. There was that ascetic touch about him. He looked like the kind of young man who would fast or gladly suffer, or crawl to a shrine on his knees. But there was something else in that handsome young face and the way he stood—a hint of dissoluteness.

"I want to know something," she said. But she looked straight ahead and neither Allie nor Brother Anthony knew to whom the inquiry was directed. And neither seemed interested anymore in any dissemination of knowledge.

Didi stood up quickly. "Yes! I want to know something!" This time she was shouting. And she pulled the spade from the ground and flung it with both hands as far as she could into the dense corn.

Then she approached Brother Anthony with such determination that the young man flinched and pulled back, looking to Allie for protection.

Didi stopped two feet from him.

"Tell me why Brother Samuel hung her body on a fence, like a scarecrow."

He didn't answer.

"Don't you hear me?" she demanded threateningly.

"I don't know what you're talking about."

"I will repeat it for you. He hung Mary Hyndman on a fence after he shot her. So all could see."

Brother Anthony's pale face had broken out in sweat. He raised his hands, uncomprehendingly. Then asked: "Why would he do that?"

"Yes! That is my question! Why would he do that!"

"It . . . is . . . inconceivable to me . . . that Brother Samuel . . . would do such . . . a horrible thing." He articulated the words very slowly.

Didi stared at him with a kind of wonder. This Brother Anthony was obviously a fool's fool. The realization deflated her anger.

He had been forced to participate in a vile scheme that involved extortion and murder. And now he was praising the man who had ensnared him—Brother Samuel.

Didi pursed her lips, trying to bring back the memory of the man. She had met him only three or four times at the monastery, but she recalled that Brother Thomas had prized him highly.

Yes, now she could see him more clearly in her mind's eye—bald, stout, very happy, very solid and trustworthy. He had been an advertising executive. He was in charge of the monastery's horticultural activities—whether food or flowers.

Why do cherubic men so often turn out to be at least a trifle satanic?

At least this Brother Anthony, standing in front of her, was not cherubic. He was too angular, too handsome, almost too beautiful to be anything but evil.

Didi laughed to herself. The night was beginning to unhinge her. She was becoming enamored of devils.

It was Allie who broke that strange spell. He tugged at her arm. "I have to talk to you a minute," he said. "Alone."

Didi nodded.

"I'm going to put Brother Anthony in the car and lock him in. Wait for me here."

Didi had no idea what Allie wanted to talk about.

Allie returned quickly and asked: "Are you okay, Didi?"

"Of course I'm okay."

"Good. Because you have to clear up a few things for me. I'm kind of confused. . . . No! I'm damned confused."

"He laid it all out for you, Allie. You heard every word."

"I don't care what he said. It has to have some bearing on reality. You can confess to murdering Batman. Or Superman. Or Bugs Bunny. That ain't reality."

"What confuses you, Allie?" she asked. She didn't want to argue with him. She didn't want to do anything but go home, take a shower, and go to sleep.

"If this whole thing was about extorting money, Didi . . . where is the evidence?"

"What kind of evidence?"

"Evidence of violence. Extortion means violence. It means threat of violence. But, Didi, I don't remember any reports from old ladies saying monks were extorting them for money . . . that monks were kidnapping their dogs. If it was a pattern of extortion there had to be complaints. There had to be reports. *There had to be something.*"

"Isn't murder violence? Mary Hyndman was murdered."

"Yes. But I mean short of murder. Murder is final. Extortion means a pattern. A continuing pattern."

"Do you want me to give you a scenario of extortion?"

"Very much so. If you can."

"I damn well can, Officer Voegler. I am a sick old woman."

"Say what?"

"I'm laying out the plot for you, Allie. I'm a sick old woman—get it?"

"Okay. I'll buy that. You're a sick old woman."

"My relatives and husband and pets are dead. I have heard of the wonderful German shepherds from Alsatian House. How they are companions in the best sense of the word. What do I do, Allie?"

"Write a letter?"

"Yes. I write a very sad letter to the Alsatian House asking to be considered for one of the dogs. I also tell them in the letter that I am poor. But I am not poor at all. I have assets. I am just being prudent. Old women tend to be that way. They act feebler and poorer than they are."

"So then what?"

"I am visited by a charming young monk. Brother Neil perhaps. He tells me my request for a dog is being considered. He is here, he says, to check out my suitability to have such an animal. I ask him how much the dog will cost if I am approved. Brother Neil says there is no charge for the placement. People traditionally just make a small donation. I am very relieved. I answer all his questions. I tell him about my assets. I tell him about my life. He makes three visits. And on the fourth visit he tells me I have been selected to receive a puppy. He delivers the dog a few days later and I give a small donation to the monastery."

"All this I understand," Allie said testily.

Didi ignored him. She continued the story at her own weary pace. "Suddenly the dreary loneliness of my life has been transformed. I have a companion. I have a protector. I love the dog. The dog loves me. I even begin to take long walks . . . to bake . . . to contact people I have avoided for years."

Didi paused and pulled up a weed. She tore it to pieces and let the pieces flutter to the ground.

Then she continued, her voice lower. Allie leaned closer.

"One day," she went on, "the young kindly monk reappears. I tell him how happy I am with the dog. Brother Neil compliments me at how well I am taking care of the animal. Then he tells me a sad story about how Alsatian House needs money desperately or it might have to close. He wonders if I could sign over to Alsatian House some of my assets.

"I gently refuse. I am very sorry I told him about my assets originally, but he had asked me then on the grounds that Alsatian House doesn't like to place dogs with indigent people. After my refusal, he bids me good day and leaves.

"A week later I receive another visit from Brother Neil. He asks again for some of my money and stocks. I refuse. He tells me that if I don't cooperate he will take the dog back. I cannot believe what he is saying. I tell him he can't do that. I won't let him do that."

"Right!" Allie interrupted. "He damn well can't. You own the dog now."

"Are you sure, Allie?"

"Of course; the dog is your property now."

"How do you know that, Allie?"

"You have a bill of sale . . . don't you?"

"No. No bills of sale are issued, Allie. No fee is charged. No legal transfer or purchase ever takes place."

Allie whistled in wonder. "I wasn't aware of that."

"In addition, I was never given any papers. I don't have the dog's registration or breeding or inoculation report. I have nothing. I can't go to the police or a lawyer. I have absolutely no proof that I own the dog."

"But at least you can prove that you corresponded with Alsatian House about getting a dog," Allie offered.

"No! Don't you remember what Brother Anthony said? The names of the old women were changed on the records. There existed no record of my real name in monastery files. And all my correspondence was destroyed."

"But what about correspondence from the monastery to you?"

"There was none. Everything was done in person, by monks visiting me."

"These people are very slick."

"Yes. Slick and deadly. Let me get back to the scenario. Brother Neil leaves without making any effort to act on his threat. But the fear of losing my dog is in my heart. I realize how much I have grown to love him and need him. Life without him is almost unthinkable.

"A week later I receive another visit. It is not Brother Neil. It is a redheaded and red-bearded man. A chubby man."

"You mean this Brother Samuel—in mufti?" Allie inquired.

"Exactly. He gives me one last chance to contribute. I refuse. He tells me he will collect the dog. I become hysterical. I grab my dog and hold him close. I tell him my dog will only be taken over my dead body. He says there will be no violence. He says that the dog will accompany him of his own free will; that my beloved animal will quickly desert me to go back to Alsatian House.

"I cannot believe what he is saying. I hold my dog tighter. He goes to his car and opens the door. Then, just with one call, my dog breaks loose, trots over, and leaps happily into the car without so much as a backward glance at me.

"I realize I have lost. I run to him and beg

him to let me keep the dog. I will give him anything he wants."

"No way, Didi. The scenario breaks down here."

"Why do you say that?"

"Because you have been taking care of the dog. You have bonded with it. The dog wouldn't leave you like that."

"An ordinary animal wouldn't. But an Alsatian House dog would."

"Why?"

"Because of its training. I watched them being trained. The animals there live, sleep, eat, and train with the monks. The entire monastery constitutes a pack. That is the genius of their training. I have never seen anything like it elsewhere. The imprinting is constantly reinforced. It almost reproduces those ancient legends of men and women who are raised in wolf packs . . . who believe they are wolves. At Alsatian House one gets the impression that there is virtually no distinction between the human and the canine residents. I actually believe that an Alsatian House-trainined German shepherd will happily leave its master or mistress even five years after it is placed. Even if during that five-year period it has not once seen the monk who comes to reclaim him."

"Amazing," Allie said.

"Yes, it is."

"But the old woman in your scenario wasn't murdered."

"Of course not."

"Mary Hyndman was."

"Obviously, Allie, Mary Hyndman decided to fight back. In some very specific way she threatened the Alsatian House organization . . . their racket. Maybe she told them she was friendly with the chief of police of Hillsbrook. Maybe she told them that their conversation had been recorded. I don't know. But she grew to hate them. And she wanted to pay them back somehow."

"Brother Anthony said she threatened to go to the newspapers."

"I don't think it was only that. The threat to their organization had to be greater than that to make them murder her. I assume the state police will find out the specifics of the threat from Brother Samuel after they confront him with Brother Anthony's confession."

"It is amazing," Allie marveled, "what can be learned in a cornfield."

Didi smiled and took his hand. She corrected him gently: "It's a cornfield with tomato plants interspersed."

Chapter 16

Wynton Chung was at the wheel of his Hillsbrook squad car. Allie Voegler was in the passenger seat. It was still early in the morning. They had just transferred Brother Anthony to the lockup at the Columbia County courthouse and now they were returning to Dutchess County.

There had been one of the usual mix-ups in the paperwork and when Allie had called in to Hillsbrook to straighten it out, the chief had told him to stop at Mary Hyndman's place on the way back—there were reports of a prowler. The report had come in from the driver of a county dump truck about five in the morning. "It could have been a deer," the chief had noted. Or a scarecrow, Allie thought.

"Why did they assign the two of us to deliver that kid?" Wynton Chung asked. There was suspicion in his voice. Allie knew why. The new officer thought that he wasn't trusted alone.

"Kid?" Allie teased. "You're not that much older than Brother Anthony."

"But a lot smarter," Chung replied.

"Amen to that," Allie replied and then explained the reason he went along.

"About ten years ago, a prisoner was being transferred upstate. He broke through the wire partition, strangled the officer, took his weapon, and escaped. The car was totaled. Since then, they put in the two-cop rule."

"Was he cuffed?" Chung asked, incredulous at the story.

"Yes, he was cuffed."

"How did he break through the partition?"

"No one knows. The cop probably knew. But he was dead."

"They get him?"

"Yeah, two days later."

"One other thing, Allie."

"What?"

"Why do they always transfer prisoners so goddamn early in the morning?"

"I have no idea."

They stopped off once for coffee and drank it standing outside the vehicle. It was a lovely summer morning. The roads were ringed with trees in full leaf. Jumbles of wildflowers—yellow and purple—pushed up around their feet.

Chung blew into his coffee cup. "Do you think that kid will do much time?"

"Not if he plays his cards right. He's the only one who can really implicate that Brother Samuel. He's the only one who can make the state's case."

"If we had the death penalty, that Brother Samuel would fry," Chung noted.

"Why not? Two counts of murder one and probably twenty counts of extortion."

"They'll never get convictions on those extortion counts," Chung said.

"Why not?"

"The old ladies who paid up and kept their puppies won't say a word. And those who didn't pay up are probably dead or senile. Besides, it's the toughest case to prove—extortion. You need a wire or a paper trail . . . or better yet . . . a sting."

"Time will tell," Allie said and the moment he said those words he wished he could recall them. They were so damn official . . . ministerial . . . like he was a damn expert on something or a world-weary wise man. Damn, he liked this young Chung. He wanted to be friends with him.

They reached Mary Hyndman's place.

"Don't pull in yet," Allie said. Wynton Chung parked the police cruiser on the side of the narrow winding road and the two cops just looked the place over.

Allie could see the trampled corn. He could see the house clearly. He could see virtually all of the property except for the wooded areas.

Wynton Chung pointed a finger. "Is that the fence?"

"Yeah. That's the fence that son of a bitch hung her on. But I never saw her. Didi found her."

"Didi? Oh, that's the vet."

"Right. Deirdre Quinn Nightingale, DVM." Allie, for some reason, always loved enunciating her name and title completely. Flawlessly. As if it were a feat.

"I hear she's one of your ladies," Officer Chung said.

Allie glared angrily at his companion. What the hell did he mean by that? Then he smiled and his face softened. He remembered that once in a while rookie Chung used that big-city language. "Didi one of my ladies? That'll be the day."

"I think we better check it out," Chung said, his hand on the door.

"Yeah, in a minute," Allie replied. Chung sat back. Then he said: "If you're not up to it, I'll do it alone. Just wait here. It doesn't seem like anything."

Allie stared at the house wearily. It wasn't that he wasn't "up to it." It was just that a lot of people besides the murderous monks might believe that Mary Hyndman had hidden money. A lot of people in Hillsbrook. If that was the case, he knew what it meant. When he was a kid there was a legend that an old dairy farmer had buried gold in his cow pasture. After the man died, it became one of the chief sports of young kids to have three cans of beer and then roar onto the field in their hot rods and start digging up the whole goddamn pasture. They never found anything except the obvious.

And that was the way it was going to be with Mary Hyndman's place as long as it was unoccupied, and maybe even after that. But he couldn't tell this to Officer Wynton Chung. He wouldn't understand. He wasn't from Hillsbrook.

"Okay. Let's go," Allie said.

They left the car and walked toward the

house. There were no fresh tire marks. No sign of anyone.

Suddenly Wynton Chung began to undo the flap of his gun holster.

Allied stared at him perplexed. "Let's keep walking like nothing's the matter," Chung said dramatically under his breath.

Allie followed instructions, he didn't increase or diminish his pace but he whispered: "What do you see? What do you see?"

"I was here two days ago, Allie . . . no, three. I left that side window open about six inches. You're supposed to do that on vacated premises. Now it's all the way up."

"Right!" Allie took charge. "When we reach the porch we separate. You go left. I go right. We meet at the window. Wait until I get there."

At the porch Allie veered right and began to circle the house. All the other windows were closed. He moved slowly, carefully. He bent down once to get his weapon, then kept it close by his side, hand down. He wondered if it was that fool of a pig farmer from the Ridge—what was his name? Ledeen—that was it. This was the kind of stupid adventure Ridge People traditionally got themselves in. Searching for fool's gold all the time.

He moved silently, slowly, his steps muffled by the still dewy grass. He turned the last corner and saw Wynton Chung there, by the window, but pressed against the side of the house.

Allie stopped. Why wasn't one of them covering the front door? How stupid could they be?

Then Wynton Chung yelled: "Coming out! He's coming out!"

Allie sprinted to the window. He could see Chung brace himself, the weapon held in both hands.

A figure burst through the open window and onto the ground. Then another! And another.

Three stray dogs. One of them had a rubber toy shaped like a bone in his mouth. It squeaked every time he moved. Once they hit the ground, they reeled a bit, and then ran happily off, not paying the slightest attention to either of the police officers.

Allie glanced at Chung. The tension of the stakeout had drained the young officer, who was laughing nervously through his fear. Allie leaned against the house, watching the canine Dalton Gang vanish into the woods, tails waving above the grass.

Mrs. Tunney was so happy to have Abigail back that she served her the oatmeal first—dumping a huge ladleful into her bowl.

Charlie Gravis, who usually got the first ladle, was quite happy to break tradition that morning. He pushed his toast in front of Abigail. And Trent Tucker pushed his bacon. And soon poor Abigail was surrounded by more food than she could consume in six breakfasts.

Abigail dropped three lumps of brown sugar into the oatmeal. Then a large dollop of salted butter. Then she poured cream in.

Mrs. Tunney beamed at the preparation. It was obvious that Abigail was all right.

Their absorption in Abigail's oatmeal technique was shattered by a sudden tapping at one of the large kitchen windows.

Outside was Didi. She was tapping with one hand and pointing with another.

Charlie Gravis motioned with one finger to his chest. His gesture said: Is it me you want?

On the other side of the window, Didi nodded vigorously. She then motioned that Charlie should join her outside.

Charlie signaled back that he would be out in five minutes.

Didi gestured angrily. She meant *now.*

Charlie muttered to himself, stood up slowly, and walked out the kitchen door into the yard.

"I want to have a conversation with you," Didi said. She had just finished her morning breathing exercise.

There was something in her voice that made Charlie nervous. He looked at her critically. If she wasn't so damn testy all the time, he thought, she would be a good-looking young woman. A bit too short for his taste. And a bit too thin for his taste. And more often than not she dressed like a sheep herder.

But her face was as pretty as a picture and her short cut, thick hair just yelled out a kind of good health. It was no wonder Mrs. Tunney was always trying to make a match for her. A young woman like that shouldn't be without a man. It wasn't civilized.

Charlie ambled toward her.

"I was in town yesterday, Miss Quinn, and everybody was talking about that shoot-out in the cornfield. And about how brave you and Voegler was."

"There was no shoot-out, Charlie."

He ignored her objection. He continued: "And we heard that the troopers found all kinds of bodies buried at Alsatian House when they raided the place. And the dogs was either sick or dying. I heard they closed the whole damn place down."

"You've been hearing nonsense, Charlie. The state troopers didn't *raid* Alsatian House. They arrested one monk and charged him with the murder of Mary Hyndman and the murder of another resident of the monastery. As for the dogs, they're fine. And Alsatian House is going to be around for a lot more years."

"I'll be damned!" Charlie said. "It sure is funny how these stories get around."

"I want to talk to you about something else, Charlie."

"Yes, ma'am."

"About Harry Brown."

"Harry Brown?" He made quite a show of furrowing his brown and scratching his head. The name seemed to have some kind of ancient but very fragile relevance to himself.

"Yes. Jake Brown's boy. The one with the big horse."

Charlie nodded but was silent.

"I ran into him at the Hillsbrook Diner. Oddly enough, he was very happy to see me. Said he couldn't thank me enough."

"You don't say?" Charlie added pleasantly.

"Yes, I do say, Charlie. Now, would you like to guess what he was so thankful for?"

"I guess, Miss Quinn, for that visit you made to his place, Miss Quinn. To fix his horse up."

"Not at all, Charlie. Guess again!"

She was really angry now, he realized. He tried to stay very calm.

Didi went on. "He wanted to thank me for the medicine you delivered for me to him. He said it was wonderful. He said I was a genius and his horse lapped it all up—honey and rosemary and all!"

Charlie knew it was big trouble now.

"And Charlie," Didi continued, "he said he was lucky he had the cash on him. Because you told him I had to have cash for the medicine."

She folded her arms and waited. She looks like a bronco rider in a rodeo, Charlie thought.

"There seems to be a misunderstanding here," Charlie said.

"Well, clear it up for me, Charlie. Clear it up!"

Charlie rocked back on his heels, desperately searching his mind for something that would function as a calming agent.

"I'm waiting."

"Well, Miss Quinn," he began, "here's what happened. You remember you told me you wanted all my home medicines off your property? Well, I loaded all of it into Trent's pickup and me and Trent headed to the town dump with it. Just as we passed John Theobold's farm, you'll never guess who we saw.

"It was Harry Brown leading a very tired horse down the road. So I figured he might as well take some of my good stuff. Why pour it all into the dump? He took one or two jars. Then, because Trent Tucker and me were broke and needed gas for the pickup, I asked him to borrow a few bucks. After all, he can afford it. His daddy has all kinds of money."

Charlie paused and sucked in air before continuing. "So you see, it was all a misunderstanding. He thought I was charging him for my services, when I was just being neighborly . . . like any good neighbor. No, ma'am. The money was just a loan to get us gas to get on back here. And I'll be paying him back every penny."

The story had exhausted him. He yearned to be back in the kitchen with his oatmeal. He could see that Mrs. Tunney was standing at the window with one of her brutal "I told you so" looks.

He watched Didi stare at the ground. She didn't answer for a long time. Charlie got fidgety.

Finally she said: "So that was the way it happened, Charlie."

"Yes, ma'am."

"Just a misunderstanding."

"Yes, ma'am."

Didi laughed ruefully. "Well, Charlie, when you do return that money, be sure and thank Mr. Brown for calling me a 'genius.' You know, that's one of the many beautiful things about you, Charlie: your selflessness. Always doing the noble thing and then letting someone else take the credit."

"Well, Miss Quinn—" Charlie began.

She cut him off quickly. "Oh, no, no, no,

Charlie. No need to be modest. You just go eat your breakfast now. We have a lot of rounds to make this morning."

"I'll be ready!" Charlie almost shouted and headed back into the kitchen.

"Yes," Didi called after him cheerfully. "I'll even take you to the bank and then run you out to the Browns' place so you can return that money you borrowed."

When the door swung closed, Didi doubled over from the pain of holding back her laughter for so long.

When she was under control again, she headed toward the front of the house to turn the jeep's engine over.

Suddenly a burst of white caught her eye. She stopped. Then another snow-white flash in the morning sun. From the fringe of the pine forest.

It was a family of white tail deer, heading for the small pond. The sight of them was a beautiful ache in her heart. It was, she realized, her mother's birthday gift to her.

When the deer reached the pond they did not drink for the longest time . . . testing every shift of the wind for danger.

Didi watched them, transfixed. She felt her mother beside her, watching also.

Finally, one of the deer dipped its head low to drink. Then another.

But a second later something spooked them and they darted off—white tails up. They were all gone as quickly as they had arrived.

Didi walked toward the jeep. The moment

she turned the corner of the house she saw a strange car parked right next to hers.

No. It wasn't strange. She had seen it before.

It was the car that had carried the red-haired murderer that terrible day.

She felt the urge to run. To just turn around and run to the back of the house and across the field and into the safe arms of the pine forest.

But then she saw that the driver was Sister Ruth.

Didi's heart calmed.

In the passenger seat was none other than Brother Thomas.

And in the backseat was another individual she recognized.

She waved to the visitors and approached.

Rose Vigdor stood in front of her worktable contemplating her options. She could either use the manual saw or the power saw. She didn't like either of them. The power saw always seemed that it was about to fly off somewhere. And the manual saw cut so slowly and required such effort that her arms would cramp.

Aretha and Huck lolled on the ground beside her. They had already eaten, gone for their morning run, and were now in their morning daze.

The front and back doors of the enormous barn had been flung open and light flooded in.

Rose stepped back from the table. She stopped fretting over the saw option, because she knew that wasn't really what was on her mind. What really preyed on her mind was a colony of hornets that had made their nest high up in the barn rafters. They had appeared in the spring and their paper-thin gray nest had now grown so large as to threaten her, her dogs, and the entire bloody universe.

She didn't even like to look up at them. And sooner or later she was going to have to deal with them, particularly when she reached that part of the barn ceiling for reclamation.

She walked to the potbellied stove and took a sip of coffee from a cup on top of the stove. Then she turned to Aretha and Huck and asked: "Why me, dogs? Why have I been selected for this torment?" The dogs blinked their lazy eyes. "You don't understand," she told them. She took another sip of the coffee.

And then she steeled herself, turned around, and stared up into the ceiling. Oh my, that nest seemed to get bigger every night. Why are they so damned industrious? Why don't they take the summer off?

She knew in her heart that when all was said and done, she was going to have to drag a high ladder to that section, climb the ladder with a hose, and destroy the nest. That was inevitable. That was sad. She hadn't returned to Nature to become a hornet killer. But it would probably come down to that. A battle between her and them . . . a battle to the death.

"I am getting very melodramatic," she said to the dogs. She put the coffee cup down.

Suddenly, Aretha and Huck jumped up, growling.

Rose turned toward the barn door. It was Didi!

"I didn't even hear your car," Rose said, rushing over to greet her friend.

Aretha and Huck kept growling. "What the hell is the matter with you dogs? You know Didi!"

"I have a favor to ask," Didi said.

"Ask. But first tell me about the monastery. Trent Tucker told me you had decided to spend some time there."

"I ended up staying a couple of nights."

"How was it? How were the dogs? Who are those monks?"

"I enjoyed myself," Didi said laconically.

The dogs were growling again. Didi said: "About that favor, Rose. A friend of mind arrived without warning. Can you put him up for a few nights?"

"Sure, Didi. You know me. It's a big barn. There are a lot of alcoves. Let him just lay his sleeping bag down."

"That's kind of you. He's a bit shy. Come out with me to my car and meet him."

They walked out of the barn, followed by Aretha and Huck.

"I don't see anyone in your jeep," Rose said.

"Oh, he's there," Didi said. And she called out: "Bozo!"

Out leaped the young shepherd. Aretha and Huck went ballistic, charging the intruder. Huck overshot him and fell over. Aretha overshot him and trampled Huck. Bozo took off. Huck recovered and chased him. Huck cor-

nered him. Bozo rolled over in surrender. Aretha arrived and took matters in hand.

"*Who* is that?" an astonished Rose asked.

"That is my friend Bozo."

"Is he from Alsatian House?"

"Yes. The monks gave him to me."

"But I thought there was a long wait to get
one of their dogs."

"There is. But I did some free vet work for
them. The abbot brought the dog to me in ap-
preciation. I don't have room for him. So I
thought he could stay with you and Aretha
and Huck for a while."

"Is he afraid of hornets?"

"I don't think so."

"Then he can stay as long as he wants."

The three dogs came trotting back together,
their tongues lolling out.

"He seems to have only one problem," Didi
said.

"What?"

"He has an inordinate fondness for certain
ragged old socks."

"Well," said Rose, "let's go to my trunk in
the barn and dig him out a big juicy one."

Didi followed her friend into the barn. She
knew that Mary Hyndman would have been
very happy with Bozo's new home.

Don't miss the next
Deirdre Quinn Nightingale
mystery,
DR. NIGHTINGALE
GOES THE DISTANCE,
coming from Signet
in August, 1995.

Deirdre Quinn Nightingale, D.V.M., sauntered down the staircase. She was trying to settle on a gait, a way of moving her slender hips, that would be in keeping with the elegant dress she was wearing—a long, gauzy red number with jet beading at the neckline. Her evening slippers were rapturously delicate, hardly there at all, with towering high heels. These had belonged to her mother, one of the only two pairs of glamorous shoes her mother ever owned.

It had been a long time since Didi had dressed up like this. So long, in fact, that she had been unable to determine whether she looked great or merely passable, whether she was overdressed or underdressed. She had stood for at least half an hour staring at herself in the long bedroom mirror, turning her head this way and that, her silver earrings flicking softly against her neck with every movement.

And now, ready or not, Cinderella had to get to the ball.

She was startled to see Charlie Gravis and Mrs. Tunney waiting for her at the bottom of the stairs. Usually they stayed in their part of the house and she stayed in hers—the kitchen and hallway being neutral ground.

But it was a little silly to be surprised to find them here on her territory. After all, it wasn't as if Charlie and Mrs. Tunney and Abigail and Trent Tucker were servants; they had the right to be anywhere in the house. They were more like boarders, boarders that her mother had passed on to her. Only this was a little different from the usual boarder situation: the four of them paid no rent. Instead they did chores in exchange for their keep. That was the arrangement, at least in theory. Truth was, there always seemed to be a dozen things remaining undone around the place—a patch of garden going unweeded, a falling-down fence, a broken lamp gathering dust somewhere.

Didi had reached the bottom of the staircase now and stood before the two elder retainers.

"My, aren't you a vision, missy! You look just beautiful," Mrs. Tunney purred.

"Thank you," Didi answered, dangerously close to blushing.

"Isn't she a sight, Charlie?" Mrs. Tunney, still beaming, turned to him for confirmation.

"Oh, yes sir. Yes sir," he said, nodding. Then he moved closer to Didi and took on a confidential tone. "I thought, maybe," Charlie Gravis said, "you would want Trent and me to take you out there and then pick you up when you're finished. You know, just so's you won't have to worry about driving tonight."

In an instant Didi's shyness turned to rage. "I'm getting so sick of that kind of suggestion, Charlie. You've got something like that to say every time I leave the house these days. Just because *one* time at *one* party—my own birthday party, in fact—I had too much to drink, you keep implying that I'm some kind of lush. Some kind of fool. But if you remember, Charlie, there was good reason to get drunk that day. A terrible thing had happened. And now I'm just going out for the evening, going to a party, like a normal, responsible, human, grown-up being. *And I won't be drinking to excess, Charlie.* Understand? I've been back to old Two-Drink Didi for some time now."

He took a hurried step backward, and tried stumblingly to explain that he "didn't mean no harm," but Didi whipped past him and Mrs. Tunney, straight through the front door of the house, and did not break stride until she reached the red Jeep in the driveway. She started the engine and drove off in a welter of screeching rubber.

Once on the road she slowed down and tried to compose herself. It was pointless, just plain stupid, to get angry at Charlie Gravis. But she never seemed to learn that lesson. Yes, downright stupid—especially tonight. She wasn't going to just any old party. She was going to the annual July gala at Avignon Farms, which was always held two weeks before they shipped their horses to Saratoga for the August racing season. It was the social event of the year in Hillsbrook and the first time Didi had ever been invited.

Avignon Farms, only fifteen miles from her house, was a picture book place: freshly painted green and white buildings, snow white fences, and emerald green grass. There was a massive gravel quadrangle within the stabling area, where the outdoor summer parties were held.

Didi was not just happy to be invited—she was thrilled. First, it would give her a chance to meet the great Dr. Hull, who took care of the fine animals at Avignon Farms and was one of the most respected vets in New York state. And, she could renew her acquaintance with that lovely gnome of a man, Max, the manager of Avignon, who had been kind enough to throw some veterinary work her way when she was just starting out and needed it bad.

It was too bad that her friend Rose Vigdor had refused to accompany her. First Rose had refused on the grounds that she hadn't been invited. Didi told her it was perfectly proper for one invited guest to bring along a friend. Then Rose refused because she had nothing to wear to such a gathering. Didi told her that the rich didn't have dress codes. Then Rose refused because, she said, when she left Manhattan to embrace a rural existence, she had vowed to herself never to go to another party. To this Didi had no response.

Didi pulled into the endless stretch of parking lot and, hoping no one was watching her, broke into unabashed laughter. On all sides of her little red Jeep were very expensive vehicles: Mercedes station wagons, specially equipped Land Rovers, Lexus sports cars, even a few Porsches.

She walked slowly to the quad. It was a

lovely July night, replete with comforting warm breezes blown down from the heavens, as if the pretty full moon were cooling the surface of her cup of coffee. The night wind played with Didi's skirts, and the sounds of half a dozen conversations floated toward her. She paused for a moment by a stable wall, inhaling that gorgeous horse essence.

Didi walked on. Several long tables had been placed in the quad, all covered with linen cloths shining ghostly white in the night. Three of them were laden with food and crystal, china and silverware; the others were carefully decorated with embroidered napkins and cut flowers and pedestled dishes overflowing with glass marbles. These latter would eventually seat the happy, prosperous guests after they tired of milling about the property, sipping champagne and admiring the horses and eating too many hors d'oeuvres.

The good-looking, alert young catering staff circulated with trays of drinks and savories. Here and there the guests nodded their greetings at Didi, and she returned them, but the fact was that she hadn't yet recognized a single person at the party.

On the extreme end of the quad, near one of the small passageways which led to the feed bins, a four-piece dance band had set up, all three musicians—including the lady vocalist—dressed in tuxedos. But they were not playing at the moment, for there seemed to be some problem with their amplifier. One musician held a flashlight while the other fiddled desperately with the back of a speaker.

Didi eased herself into the party, hooking a small plate of stuffed mushrooms and a glass of white wine. She wandered about, holding the plate but not eating, sipping from the wineglass, and stepping in and out of other people's conversations.

These were bred in the bone horse people, the real item. Walking around in the heady atmosphere of horse manure and straw in their country WASP finery and their handed-down diamonds—and loving it. And all their chatter was about Sisterwoman, the unraced two-year-old filly that Avignon Farms was sending to Saratoga. She was a big bay lady—very big—out of the same lineage that had produced the great French racing mare Dahlia. People were talking about her as if she were destined to be the new Ruffian.

Didi chuckled quietly when she realized that from the center of the quad one could see the horses in their stalls, staring out on the spectacle of the party. They were like old folks in their robes on New Year's Eve, watching the Times Square festivities on TV.

Then Didi spotted the unmistakable Max; his face was so lined that a horse van might have rolled over it.

She waved to him and started over. He was standing in front of one of the stable doors, chewing on an unlit small cigar. As usual, he was dressed like an old-fashioned horseman, Mickey Rooney in *National Velvet*, right down to his knickers.

If Didi had had to guess, she wouldn't have thought that this was Max's favorite way to spend an evening. He looked terribly uncomfortable, out of place, standing in his little corner, now and again exchanging forced pleasantries with strangers, watching the party goers eat and drink.

"Can I get you a drink, Max?" she asked.

"No," he said harshly. "Had my fill of things already."

Didi stood next to him and finally sampled the canapes. The mushrooms were delicious. Max pointed out the various luminaries to her as she ate: Mr. and Mrs. Thomas Nef, the owners of Avignon Farms; Shirley Hammond, the owner of Sisterwoman; Brock Flew, the filly's trainer; and several other wealthy or infamous people. Didi now understood why she hadn't recognized the party goers when she arrived— most of them were simply not from Hillsbrook.

"Which one is Doctor Hull?" she asked.

Max looked around. "Not here yet."

"Will you introduce me to him when he gets here, Max? I feel funny just going up to him and sticking out my hand."

"Sure. But I think he probably has heard of you," Max said.

"I take that as a compliment, Max."

He bit down on his cigar and said nothing.

The band finally got its wiring problems straightened out. They were playing a Guy Lombardo medley—with the requisite amount of irony in their performance. Scattered sighs of delight were heard, and a few couples drew close to the bandstand and began to dance.

"What do you think of the filly?" Didi asked Max.

"What filly?"

"The one everybody's talking about—Sisterwoman."

"She ain't been to the races yet," said the eternally pessimistic Max.

"But she's big and she's fast and she sure has the breeding," Didi said.

"So was my cousin—but the cops got him anyway."

Didi laughed. Max was wonderful. She found herself wishing that the old horseman worked on her place instead of here.

The first gunshot splintered the air.

Didi jumped and instinctively grabbed Max's arm. Not exactly sure what they'd just heard, but wary all the same, several of the party goers fell silent, cocking their heads. It might have been a car backfiring. Amateur fireworks?

The second shot came five seconds later.

The elderly horseman took off at a run, Didi not far behind him. The music had stopped.

They ran into the aisle of the stable. The hay seemed to have taken on an acrid, burnt odor.

Max went to the stall at the north end. The gate was open.

He raised his hand as he peered in, signifying that Didi should stay back.

She ignored the gesture and stepped around him.

What she saw she would never forget.

A handsome white-haired man, about sixty-five years of age, dressed in formal attire, was seated on the floor of the stall, his back against the far wall. In the hand that rested on the straw-covered floor was a sleek automatic weapon.

A big bay filly lay on the floor as well, her head in the man's lap.

Both appeared to be dead.

Didi could see the bullet hole in the man's forehead. And there was blood all over the filly's face.

The man was Samuel Hull, D.V.M. The filly was Sisterwoman.

Shocked, whispering guests crowded into the stall behind Didi and Max.

Didi, overwhelmed by the horror of the scene, sank to her knees. She gathered straw from the stall floor and began to wipe the blood and gore from the beautiful filly's face.

An open equine eye emerged.

It was not the blank gaze of death.

It was the dilated eye of sedation.

"She's alive!" Didi shouted, jumping up and grabbing Max's arm with such force that the small man groaned.

"She's not dead, Max! She's been sedated. Help me get her up! Help me get her walking!"

Dr. Didi Quinn Nightingale, in her elegant party dress, got to work.

Be sure to read the first book in the Dr. Nightingale series:
DR. NIGHTINGALE COMES HOME

Deirdre "Didi" Quinn Nightingale needs to solve a baffling mystery to save her struggling veterinary practice in New York state. Bouncing her red Jeep along country roads, she is headed for the herd of beautiful, but suddenly very crazy, French Alpine dairy goats of a "new money" gentleman farmer. Diagnosing the goats' strange malady will test her investigative skills and win her a much needed wealthy client. But the goat enigma is just a warm-up for murder. Old Dick Obey, her dearest friend since she opened her office, is found dead, mutilated by wild dogs. Or so the local police force says. Didi's look at the evidence from a vet's perspective convinces her the killer species isn't canine but human. Now she's snooping among the region's forgotten farms and tiny hamlets, where a pretty sleuth had better tread carefully on a twisted trail of animal tracks, human lies, and passions gone deadly. . . .

And the second book:
DR. NIGHTINGALE
RIDES THE ELEPHANT

Excitement is making Deirdre "Didi" Nightingale, D.V.M., feel like a child again. There'll be no sick cows today. No clinic. No rounds. She is going to the circus. But shortly after she becomes veterinarian on call for a small traveling circus, Dolly, an extremely gentle Asian elephant, goes berserk and kills a beautiful dancer before a horrified crowd. Branded a rogue, Dolly seems doomed, and in Didi's opinion it's a bum rap that shouldn't happen to a dog. Didi is certain someone tampered with the elephant and is determined to save the magnificent beast from being put down. Her investigation into the tragedy leads her to another corpse, an explosively angry tiger trainer, and a "little people" performer with a big clue. Now, in the exotic world of the Big Top, Didi is walking the high wire between danger and compassion . . . knowing that the wild things are really found in the darkness, deep in a killer's twisted mind.